Match Wits with Super Sleuth Nancy Drew!

Collect the Original
Nancy Drew Mystery Stories®
by Carolyn Keene

Available in Hardcover!

Celebrate 60 Years with the World's Best Detective!

THE DOUBLE JINX MYSTERY

A bird of ill omen is mysteriously left on the Drews' front lawn. Did the person who put it there do so with the intent of jinxing Nancy and her father?

This strange incident involves Nancy in her famous lawyer-father's case concerning a rare bird farm threatened with destruction to make room for a high-rise apartment house complex. Persons opposed to the ruthless take-over of the farm are being made the frightened victims of jinxing by bad luck symbols and other threats to their safety. Even Nancy and her friend Ned Nickerson become targets!

Nancy soon realizes that helping honest people to overcome their superstitions and fears can be as challenging as tracking down criminals. The young detective's thrilling adventures will keep the reader in breathless suspense from the first page to the last.

"The symbol is a jinx!" Mrs. Thurston said.

The Double Jinx Mystery

BY CAROLYN KEENE

GROSSET & DUNLAP
Publishers • New York
A member of The Putnam & Grosset Group

PRINTED ON RECYCLED PAPER

Contents

CHAPTER		PAGE
I	BOMB THREAT?	1
II	BIRD OF ILL OMEN	10
III	KAMMY'S ESP	18
IV	SUSPICIOUS DIGGING	28
V	A CRIMINAL'S IDENTITY	36
VI	A NEW WORRY	47
VII	LEAPING SPECTER	54
VIII	UNSEEN VISITOR	61
IX	THE PUZZLING CIRCLE	69
X	UNPLEASANT COUNCILMAN	79
XI	MISSING PET	89
XII	THE DOUBLE JINX	98
XIII	A NEAR CAPTURE	108
XIV	STRANGE HIDING PLACES	118
XV	FINGERPRINT PROOF	125
XVI	NANCY'S STRATEGY	134
XVII	FRIGHTENING PLUNGE	141
XVIII	AN ARREST	152
XIX	LOST LOOT	161
XX	A SPOOK UNSPOOKED	171

The
Double
Jinx
Mystery

CHAPTER I

Bomb Threat?

NANCY Drew sat crosslegged on her bed. George Fayne sprawled on the floor. Bess Marvin had draped herself in a flowered chair and dangled her legs over one arm.

"Let's review this mystery," suggested Nancy, an attractive girl of eighteen with blue eyes and reddish-blond hair.

"Great idea," George replied. She had a boyish figure and short dark hair. "You haven't told us one word about it except that your father has been engaged to unjinx a man."

"How can a lawyer or anyone else do that?" asked Bess, plump, pretty, and blond. "I've heard that if a person is jinxed, he'll have bad luck the rest of his life." Bess shifted her position and swung her legs over the other arm of the chair. "I sure hope no one ever jinxes me!"

Nancy smiled. "Nix to jinx. But seriously, Dad

was warned by phone that if he took this case, the caller would put a curse on him."

"That's ridiculous!" George burst out. "Of course your father doesn't believe that anyone could do such a thing."

"He's not superstitious, but he can't shrug off a threat of injury," Nancy replied.

She told her friends that her father's client, a man named Oscar Thurston, lived outside Harper, a few miles away. He had been threatened several times by unknown persons.

"Dad thinks it's because Mr. Thurston won't sell his farm," Nancy explained. "It's not an ordinary farm. He has a small zoo and several huge cages of birds. Many of the birds are rare and very beautiful, Dad says."

George frowned. "If Mr. Thurston doesn't want to sell, okay. He doesn't have to. What's this about his being jinxed?"

Nancy's reply made George frown deeper. "A firm, called the High Rise Construction Company, is determined to get his land and build apartment buildings on it as part of a large complex. The owner has asked the town council to have the Thurston place condemned."

Bess looked indignant. "Sounds pretty unfair. Can't Mr. Thurston stop them?"

"Dad is trying to," Nancy said, "but he has been so busy with other cases, he hasn't been able to do much investigating yet."

George grinned. "You called Bess and me to be on standby in case your dad asks you to help solve the mystery of the jinx."

"Right," said Nancy.

At that moment the front doorbell rang. Nancy hurried down the stairs to answer it. When she opened the door, no one was there. "Maybe Dad ordered something delivered from a store," she said to herself. Stepping outside, she looked for a package but none was in sight.

"Who could have rung the bell?" she wondered.

As she glanced up and down the block, Nancy caught sight of a strange-looking bird. It was standing motionless on the lawn across from the circular driveway which led from the house to the street. The bird was about seven inches long. It had a speckled breast, variegated shades of white, brown and gray on its back, and a soft tail. Most noticeable was the peculiar way its neck was twisted and its drooping head turned backwards.

Curious to know what had detained Nancy, Bess and George and Hannah Gruen, the Drews' housekeeper, had come outside. Motherly, middle-aged Mrs. Gruen had lived with Nancy and her father Carson Drew, a River Heights attorney, since the death of Mrs. Drew when Nancy was three years old.

"Who rang the bell?" Hannah asked.

"I don't know," Nancy replied, "but I guess he or she left that bird." She walked over to it. As

Nancy stooped to pick up the bird, she burst out laughing. "It's a stuffed or mounted one!"

"Stuffed?" Bess repeated. "Why would anyone leave you this—this— What is it?"

Hannah knew the answer because the study of birds was her hobby. "The bird is a breed of woodpecker rarely seen in our country. It's a wryneck and comes from the Eurasian area of Europe."

George looked at the bird closely. "It certainly doesn't resemble our downy woodpeckers. Say, why would the person who left this run away?"

"Yes, why?" Bess put in. "Must be something weird about it."

"Wrynecks," said Hannah, "were used in witchcraft to put jinxes on people."

"Jinxes?" Nancy repeated, startled. Instantly she set the bird down and motioned everyone away from the wryneck. She rushed into the house, exclaiming, "There may be a bomb in the bird! I'll phone the police!"

Within minutes after her call a squad car arrived. Two of the four men were bomb experts who identified themselves as Mercer and Zender. They immediately tested the wryneck. The others stood at a safe distance waiting for the answer.

"There's nothing suspicious about this bird," one of them said. "Have you any idea who left it here?"

Nancy shook her head but mentioned the mysterious ringing of the Drews' front doorbell.

"There may be a bomb in the bird!"
Nancy exclaimed.

Then she added, "I understand this is a wryneck. These birds were used to put jinxes on superstitious people."

"That's right," the man replied. "The question is, was the bird left here as a warning and is it intended for you three girls or for the Drew family?" He looked directly at Nancy. "Has your father acquired any enemies lately?"

Nancy felt that she should not mention her father's newest case nor the warning telephone call. She merely said, "You know how persistent and thorough my father is. When he begins hunting for the truth, he usually makes an enemy of someone on the opposing side of the case he's handling."

Mercer asked if she knew anybody who might be playing a joke on her. Again Nancy's answer was no.

The officers declared there was nothing more they could do and the men said good-by. After they had driven off, Nancy and the others examined the wryneck. There were no identification marks on the bird, the young detective observed.

Hannah asked, "Nancy, what do you want to do with this bird?"

"I think I'll call Dad and ask him. It's just possible he'll know something about it."

She phoned Mr. Drew but he too was puzzled why the wryneck had been left on their lawn.

"Take the bird inside and keep it," he said. "Nancy, you ought to be able to track down the owner. But in the meantime I have another job for you. Could you get hold of Bess and George and drive out to Mr. Thurston's farm?"

Nancy laughed. "They're here now, so we can start right off. I'd like to meet Mr. and Mrs. Thurston. Any instructions?"

Her father said the assignment was to check the farm carefully for anything that seemed suspicious or underhanded on the part of the High Rise Construction Company.

"I understand from their bank that they're a reputable outfit. But look for surveyor's stakes that might have been pounded into the fields or marks put on the fences or trees."

"All right, Dad. See you later."

Immediately Nancy relayed her father's request. "How about it, girls?"

George answered, "At your service."

Nancy brought her convertible from the garage and the other two girls climbed in. On the way to the Thurstons, Bess said, "Tell us more about this High Rise deal."

Nancy said she had not seen the place, but the idea of destroying the bird farm and ousting the Thurstons was abhorrent to her.

"Dad says that the school children and grownups from the town of Harper and for miles around go there in busloads to see the animals, and the birds particularly. It would be a shame to deprive all those people of something so enjoyable and educational."

George asked, "Who will decide all this?"

"Presumably the town council," Nancy replied. "Dad told me that the five councilmen have been approached one by one by the staff of the High Rise Construction Company. They are trying to persuade them to vote against Mr. Thurston because of a great need for housing developments."

George set her jaw. "And probably trying to bribe the councilmen," she said.

Bess looked at her cousin disapprovingly. "Why do you always have to be so suspicious?" she asked. "Nancy, what do you think?"

The young detective smiled. "Remember what the law says: A man is presumed to be innocent until he is proved guilty."

George made no comment.

Nancy had been watching road signs and presently turned into a side street of Harper and drove all the way to the end. A neat sign at the entrance to a farm said:

Oscar Thurston's Zoo and Aviary
Visitors Welcome

A tree-shaded driveway led to the house and other buildings. Nancy parked and the three girls stepped out.

"Isn't this beautiful?" Bess burst out. Some distance back of the large, attractive old-fashioned farmhouse was a long row of huge wire cages. "Let's look at the birds before we introduce ourselves," she begged.

Nancy and George nodded and the girls headed for the end cage. Before they reached it, Nancy suddenly gasped in astonishment.

"What's the matter?" Bess asked.

Nancy whispered, "There's a man with wire clippers snipping the cage!"

"The birds will get out!" George exclaimed. "There's a good-sized hole!"

"We must stop him!" Nancy urged, and started to run toward the man.

At that moment he looked up and saw her coming toward him, followed by Bess and George. Instantly he stopped work and sped away in the opposite direction across a field, carrying the clippers.

"We must catch him!" Nancy said tensely. "George, you come with me. Bess, will you try to block up that hole so no birds can get out?"

The race after the fleeing figure began.

CHAPTER II

Bird of Ill Omen

THOUGH Nancy and George ran as fast as they could, the stranger who had snipped the wire cage outdistanced them. Apparently he was familiar with the territory. He had skirted the rough terrain, but the girls had to watch constantly for stones and pits. They finally stopped, out of breath, their faces flushed pink from the exertion.

"It's a shame he got away," George said in disgust.

Nancy was more optimistic. "At least we can give a good description of him. Let's check. He had a long thin nose and dark squinty eyes."

George nodded. "And a full reddish beard."

"He was of medium height," Nancy added.

George chuckled. "And he wore sports clothes that looked too large for him."

The girls trudged back toward the cage where they had left Bess. In the meantime she had been breaking branches off a nearby tree and stuffing them into the hole. Some of the larger birds in the cage that looked like hawks began to squawk loudly. Realizing she was a stranger and about to cut off their chance for freedom, they made an earsplitting racket.

"Oh be quiet!" Bess ordered. The birds, however, paid no attention to the command.

In a few moments the squawking brought a muscular-looking man on the run from a barn back of the cages. He was dressed in a coverall and Bess was sure he worked at the Thurston farm.

"What's going on here?" he thundered at her. "And what are you trying to do to that cage?"

Bess was frightened. She asked, "Are you Mr. Thurston?"

"No, I'm not," the man replied. "My name's Rausch. I work for Mr. Thurston. Well, young lady, are you going to answer my questions?"

Quickly Bess told him of seeing a man cutting the wire cage. "When he spotted me and my friends he ran away. They went after him. I stayed to plug this hole. That's what I'm doing."

"A likely story," Rausch replied. "I think you're connected with those people who are trying to drive Mr. Thurston away from here."

"I am not! If I were, I certainly wouldn't be standing here and trying to explain!" She was no longer afraid of the man—merely angry.

Bess's face reddened as Nancy and George, who

were hurrying back, saw her talking heatedly to the man. Every once in a while he would shake his finger at her.

"Something's wrong!" Nancy exclaimed and started to run, with George keeping pace alongside her.

When they reached the cage, Bess said, "Girls, tell this man what we saw. He won't believe me. And guess what? He thinks I'm connected with people who are trying to run Mr. Thurston off his property!"

George's eyes blazed. "That's ridiculous—utterly ridiculous," she cried out. "Incidentally, who are you?"

Bess replied, "He says he works for Mr. Thurston."

"Then I suggest," said Nancy, "that everyone calm down."

She told him about the man clipping the wire cage and the chase. She ended by saying, "We didn't capture him, but we have a good description of him. Do you know anybody who's of medium height, has a long thin nose, dark squinty eyes, a full reddish beard, and wears oversized sport clothes?"

The expression on Rausch's face changed instantly. "I guess you girls are telling the truth and I'm sorry I spoke to you harshly, miss," he said to Bess. "I don't know anyone who fits that description."

Rausch then said he would go for some material with which to mend the fence. "Will you girls please stay here a few moments longer until I get back? Don't let any of these birds fly out!" he said, hurrying off.

When Rausch returned, Nancy asked if the girls could help him. "Well, yes, you can," he answered. "These birds may think I'm here to feed them and fly through this hole before I can get it covered." He said to Bess, "Your idea of putting branches in there was good." He now removed them.

Bess smiled.

A new piece of steel cable was fitted into the section that had been cut out. Then, as the girls held it tightly against the opening, Rausch quickly threaded a wire in and out, weaving the two sections together firmly.

"We came to see the Thurstons," Nancy told him.

When the job was finished, he took the girls to the rear door of the farmhouse and ushered them inside.

"Please wait here a minute," he said. "Mrs. Thurston is a semi-invalid and sometimes she doesn't feel well enough to have visitors."

He disappeared toward the front of the house, but presently came back with a ruddy-faced, jolly-looking man. His graying black hair had receded from his forehead a couple of inches.

"Oscar," said Rausch, "these are the girls who came to see you. And they'll tell you what happened at one of the cages. I must go out now and tend to the animals."

He hurried off as Nancy introduced herself, Bess, and George.

"How do you do?" Mr. Thurston said. He looked at Nancy, "You are Carson Drew's daughter?"

Nancy nodded. "Dad has told me about taking your case. He asked me to come out and meet you and look around your place."

"I'm pretty proud of my birds," said their owner. "By the way, call me Oscar. Everybody does. I'm sorry Mrs. Thurston isn't quite ready for visitors. Come outside. I'll tell you something about my birds."

On the way to the cages, Nancy briefed him about the wire snipper. Oscar remarked, "One more bit of harassment. I don't know how much your father has told you about the trouble here, but I'm being bothered all the time in one way or another—threats, the warning of a curse to be put on me, and jinxes on my birds."

Nancy told him that she knew about the housing development to be built by the High Rise Construction Company and that Oscar did not want to sell his property.

"That's right," he said. "And my wife adores

this place. She isn't very well and I'm afraid that if we had to move out and leave all this it would be very bad for her health."

"Tell me some more about what has been happening to you," Nancy requested.

"About a week ago," Oscar replied, "a stink bomb was tossed through an open window. We had to get out of the house for one whole day."

"How ghastly!" Bess put in.

"Yes, it was," Oscar went on. "A few days ago I received an unsigned note in the mail. It said, 'You're holding up the chance for your neighbors to make a lot of money. Sell out or you will regret it!' "

"Where is the note?" Nancy asked.

"My wife found it and threw the note away."

George frowned. "Do the police know about this?"

Oscar shook his head. "I had left everything to Mr. Drew."

Bess smiled. "Nancy will never tell you, but she's an amateur detective. Sometimes she works with her father and has solved lots of cases. She lets George and me help her and it's pretty exciting. Recently we all worked on a really spooky one, *The Secret of Mirror Bay*."

Oscar's eyes opened wide. "I'm glad you told me. Nancy, I believe you and your friends have a real mystery to solve right here. Well, let's start with my telling you something about the birds."

He led the girls to a cage that contained many varieties of woodpeckers.

"There's a joke about these birds," he told them. "It's said they live an upright life. You notice how each one stands erect on the trunk of a tree. These birds can do this because they have short legs and toes that are strong and tipped with sharp, curved nails. Two of the toes face forward, the others to the side. In this way they can cling to the bark.

"Besides, they have pointed tails with a stiff strong shaft which they use for propping themselves against the trunk. If you look closely, you will see that a woodpecker's bill is straight, hard, and comes to a point. It certainly makes an ideal digging tool to get the insects from the bark. By the way, the constant pounding would probably make the birds ill if they didn't have very strong skulls to take up the shock."

The three girls listened intently, taking in all these details.

Oscar said, "I suppose you can't see their tongues, but they're long and the birds can stick them out to an astonishing length beyond their bills. Since the tongue has backward-pointing barbs at the tip"—Oscar smiled—"it's bad news for an insect that gets caught in it."

The naturalist farmer moved on to a smaller cage.

Immediately Bess cried out, "It's a wryneck!"

Oscar looked at her in amazement. "Few people know about this type of woodpecker. How did you learn about it?"

Bess looked at Nancy, not knowing if she should tell the story of the stuffed wryneck left on the Drews' lawn.

Nancy did not answer the question directly. She asked, "Where did you get this bird?"

"It belongs to a girl who is attending Harper University in town here," Oscar replied. "She's a Eurasian and brought this pet from Europe. She is staying with us."

Nancy was startled. Could there be any connection between the girl and the person who had left the wryneck at the Drew house?

CHAPTER III

Kammy's ESP

WHILE Nancy was wondering about the Eurasian girl's connection with the mystery, Oscar said, "Our visitor's name is Kamenka. We call her Kammy for short. She is a fine girl, but a bit mysterious at times. You must meet her." He looked at his watch. "She will be home soon. Can you wait and see her?"

"Yes," Nancy replied, eager to meet the owner of the wryneck. "Bess and George, you're not in a hurry, are you?"

"No," the cousins replied.

Oscar pointed out that the wryneck differed from other woodpeckers in the way it sat on a tree. "You will notice that Petra—that's the bird's name—perches on a branch like other breeds of birds and never clings upright to the trunk of a tree. This type of woodpecker does not peck or bore for food but picks it up mostly from the surface of the ground. He eats flying insects and will often make a short dash into the air to catch one."

By the time Oscar and the girls reached the house, Mrs. Thurston was ready to receive the callers. Though she was in a wheelchair, the invalid managed to propel herself around rather quickly. She was thin and frail looking.

After greeting the girls, she said, "My husband doesn't like me to sit in the wheelchair, but he doesn't realize how weak I am from worry."

Mrs. Thurston went on to talk about the Thurstons' problem.

"Isn't it dreadful?" she said. "Oscar and I have been here for many years and built up this place. Why does anyone have a right to make us sell it?"

"There, there, Martha," Oscar said soothingly. "Please don't get yourself so excited. Nancy Drew and her father are going to straighten everything out for us."

"Oh I hope so," his wife replied.

Suddenly she changed the subject and asked the girls if they had seen the owls and the ravens.

"Not yet," Nancy replied.

"Oscar," Mrs. Thurston said, "would you go and make some tea for us and serve cookies with it?"

Her husband left the room. Then Mrs. Thurston said, "You know, girls, that if an owl continually hoots in a tree near your home, it's an omen of ill health for you. I keep telling Oscar he should get rid of our owls."

Nancy said gently, "I'm sure there's no truth in the superstition. Don't let the owls bother you."

Bess and George supported their friend's comment but Mrs. Thurston paid no attention.

"Those ravens out in their cage bring trouble, too," she went on. "With them around there's always danger of a libel suit."

Further attempts to dissuade Mrs. Thurston failed. Finally Nancy said, "Tell us about some of the good birds out in your cages."

Martha Thurston relaxed. "Well, doves bring peace, and robins are messengers of good luck. My favorite birds are the darling little hummingbirds. They are most amazing creatures."

"In what way?" George asked.

The woman warmed to her subject. "I like to think of them as miniature helicopters. They can hover motionless, and believe it or not, fly backwards.

"Those beautiful little iridescent birds—which by the way are only three and three-quarter inches long—have the most amazing energy. I understand that for their size, they can outperform any living warm-blooded animal. When a hummingbird is hovering he has an energy output per unit of weight ten times that of a man who is running nine miles an hour."

The three girls were intensely interested to learn this and waited for Mrs. Thurston to go on.

"Do you know what the daily output of energy for a man is?"

When the girls shook their heads, she said, "It's thirty-five hundred calories. But listen to this. The daily output of a hummingbird if calculated in the terms of a hundred-and-seventy-pound man is equivalent to a hundred and fifty-five thousand calories?"

"Wow!" George exclaimed. She grinned. "Hereafter I'll have more admiration for hummingbirds."

By this time Oscar had the tea service and a platter of cookies ready. He wheeled them in on a small cart which he set in front of his wife. She thanked him and then began to pour the tea.

Just as everyone had been served, Kamenka came in and was introduced. A combination of European and Asian features gave her an unusual beauty. Her complexion was olive. She had high cheekbones and straight black hair. Kammy did not look at the girls unpleasantly but did not smile either. The slightly dark shadows under her eyes gave the Eurasian young woman a rather mysterious, troubled expression.

"How did your class in ornithology go today?" Mrs. Thurston asked her.

"Very well, thank you. Sometimes I find it hard to understand the English. The scientific Latin terms are easier for me."

Bess spoke up. "Ornithology is the study of birds, isn't it?"

Kammy smiled and opened her big brown eyes wide. Nancy was startled by the change in the girl's appearance. Now she looked happy!

Kammy laughed lightly. "I hardly expect to cover the whole subject," she said. "If I knew half as much as Oscar does, I could get a master's degree."

The Eurasian girl now seemed quite charming. She took a cup of tea and a cookie and sat down with the others.

"I am hoping," she said, "that I may remain in America, but I am afraid that the way my student visa reads, I'll have to return to my native land."

Oscar said he would miss Kammy very much. "She is a wonderful help to Mrs. Thurston and me. She knows how to take care of the birds and animals as well as Rausch and I do."

Nancy asked her if she went to the university museum often.

"Oh yes," Kammy replied. "I study the birds and animals in the glass cases. But I would rather watch the live ones. This is the very best place I could be." She smiled at Oscar.

Bess stood up and set down her teacup and saucer. She turned to Kammy. "In your country do some people use wrynecks to cast spells on other persons?"

Suddenly Kammy's happy expression became sullen. She too arose and put down her teacup.

Without answering Bess's question, she said, "Will you all please excuse me? I'd like to go to my room." She picked up her handbag and the books she had brought with her, and left the room.

"Oh dear!" said Bess. "I'm afraid I hurt Kammy's feelings but I didn't mean to."

Mrs. Thurston spoke up. "Don't worry about it. Kammy is moody. By the way, she's also very psychic—knows a lot about astrology."

Oscar laughed. "At least my wife thinks she does. She insists that Kammy can tell from the stars exactly what's going to happen to you."

Nancy smiled and said to him, "Has Kammy predicted the outcome of the land deal?"

"Oh yes," Mrs. Thurston answered, "but she won't tell us, so I'm afraid it's bad."

Nancy stood up and said the girls must leave. "I'd like to walk over the fields before driving home." She thanked the Thurstons for their hospitality and assured them that she would help her father as much as possible to solve the mystery.

Bess and George followed the young detective

over the hundred-acre property, looking for evidence that the proposed builders had driven stakes to indicate a road or a building. Nancy concentrated on trees and large stones for any paint marks. They found nothing.

Finally Nancy said, "Evidently the High Rise people haven't done any surveying yet. I'm glad. Well, let's go!"

On the drive home the three girls talked about their unusual visit. They could not dismiss their mixed feelings about Mrs. Thurston and Kammy. There was no question in their minds but that Oscar was a fine man.

"He's not superstitious," said Bess. "But his wife certainly is. I'll bet that's what keeps her from getting better."

"You're probably right," George added. "And Kammy certainly is hypersensitive."

Nancy dropped George and Bess at their homes, then started for her own. She suddenly recalled having promised Hannah Gruen she would stop at the supermarket to buy some groceries and meat.

She parked and entered the huge market. Nancy took one of the carts and started on her errands. She had it almost filled when suddenly there was a rumble behind her. Turning, she was just in time to see a fast-oncoming cart. It whacked her ankle.

"Oh!" she cried out in pain.

Nancy looked up to see who was responsible but no one was in sight. She was sure that someone had deliberately tried to injure her!

Nancy glanced down and was dismayed to see blood on her leg. Quickly she tied a couple of clean tissues around her ankle and decided to go directly home.

She rolled the cart to the checkout counter, paid for the groceries, and hobbled to the parking lot. Nancy put the packages inside the car, then climbed in. Worried that she might be harmed again, Nancy locked the doors and started off. She detected nobody watching her, and no car followed her out of the parking lot.

Hannah was not at home. Nancy put her packages on the kitchen table and went at once to the second floor. She removed her makeshift bandage and her shoe, then bathed the wound with an antiseptic.

Nancy finished the first-aid treatment just as the telephone rang. She was surprised to find that the caller was Mrs. Thurston.

"Nancy, did you have an accident on the way home?" the woman asked.

"Why yes, I did—a little one," she replied, and told what had happened to her.

"Kammy knew it. Her ESP was working! She came rushing to me a little while ago and said, 'I just had a strange vibration that Nancy Drew has been hurt!' "

The young detective was amazed. Maybe Kammy did have some kind of exceptional sensitivity.

Nancy merely said, "Kammy is psychic all right but please tell her I'll be okay."

Mrs. Thurston suggested that Nancy tell Kammy herself. When the Eurasian girl came to the phone, she said she was glad to hear Nancy had not been seriously injured.

"I want to apologize for my behavior this afternoon. Perhaps someday I can tell you more about myself, but Bess's remark upset me a bit. Please give her a message: that I hold no resentment and I would like very much to be friends with you three girls."

Nancy told her that Bess felt bad about hurting Kammy's feelings and certainly would not do it again.

The two talked a little longer, then said goodby. A few minutes later Mr. Drew, tall, handsome and distinguished looking, arrived home. He and Nancy sat down in the living room to talk. She gave him a full report on her trip to the Thurston farm. "We couldn't find anything suspicious."

"What happened to your ankle?" he asked.

"Oh it's nothing," Nancy insisted, and told how the accident had occurred.

The lawyer frowned. "You remember I've been

threatened. Now my enemy may have become yours also. Please, dear, watch carefully wherever you go."

Nancy promised to be cautious. Then her father leaned forward and said, "Nancy, I have something startling to tell you."

CHAPTER IV

Suspicious Digging

SITTING forward on her chair, Nancy waited eagerly for her father's startling news.

He smiled. "I did a little investigating myself today, and found out the wryneck was stolen. Can you guess from where?"

"Some museum, I suppose," Nancy replied. "But that would not be startling."

"The bird was taken from the Harper University Museum!"

"Near the Thurstons' farm?"

Mr. Drew nodded. The lawyer's eyes twinkled. "Nancy, you're not the only one who gets hunches. I had one and called several museums until I located the right one. The curator was surprised when I told him the bird had been left here. Nancy, didn't you say that the Eurasian girl who is living with the Thurstons is studying ornithology at Harper University?"

Nancy knew at once what her father was thinking. "Surely Kammy didn't steal it from the museum!" she exclaimed. "Why, she'd be the last one in the world to do that. She's a dedicated student."

Mr. Drew shrugged. "What you say is logical, Nancy, but don't forget that sometimes a person lets superstition and custom take precedence over his good sense. Other people must be tolerant about this."

Nancy thought about this comment for several seconds and had to admit that this was an example of her father's wise counseling which had made him one of the leading attorneys in the state.

He changed the subject. "Nancy," he said, "will you please take the wryneck back to the university museum? I talked with Professor Saunders there and told him I would see that the bird was returned soon."

"I'll go first thing tomorrow morning," Nancy replied. "Perhaps Kammy will be there and I'll have a chance to talk to her."

Unfortunately the Eurasian girl was not at the university the next morning. To Nancy's disappointment she learned from the registrar that Kammy had no classes all day.

"Oh well." Nancy sighed and decided to seek out Professor Saunders. He proved to be a very pleasant man and thanked Nancy profusely for returning the stolen wryneck.

"I can't understand it," he said. "The only person who has a key to the glass cases besides myself is our maintenance man. He has been here many years and is entirely trustworthy."

Nancy suggested that someone might have used a skeleton key. "Have you any idea who?"

He shook his head in bewilderment. "If a person really wanted to get money for the collection, he would have had to steal many birds. Why he only picked out the wryneck is a mystery to me."

"I think it was to jinx us Drews," Nancy replied. "Fortunately, we don't believe in such things. Nevertheless, we'd like to find out who did it. There was no note or any clue to the person who brought it."

"That must make you feel a bit uncomfortable," Saunders commented.

Nancy asked the professor if he or the maintenance man ever lent their keys to anyone to borrow birds for study or exhibition purposes.

"Sometimes I do when I'm too busy to leave my office," he answered. "But only to graduate students—and on occasion, other professional ornithologists. I jot down their names and requests. That way I don't have to depend on my memory."

"Has anyone asked you in the past week or so for the keys to the cases?" Nancy queried.

Professor Saunders thought for a minute, then said, "Yes, three graduate students have asked for the keys recently but all returned them as soon as possible and brought back the birds to me personally."

Nancy was puzzled. Someone had apparently removed the mounted wryneck from the case without breaking either the lock or the glass. Who was it and how did he do it?

"Would you mind telling me the names of the students and which birds they borrowed?" she asked.

The professor took a notebook from his pocket and flipped the pages. "I see that one boy took a quail. A girl student studied a flycatcher. Oh, yes, and one did want the wryneck."

"Was it Kamenka?" Nancy asked eagerly, and mentioned her brief introduction to the student.

"Yes, but I assure you she returned it. Anyway, what reason would she have for stealing the bird and leaving it on your lawn?"

Nancy smiled. "I can't figure out a single reason."

She was thinking, however, that for some purpose not clear yet, Kammy might have taken the bird out.

"But I hate to be suspicious of her," the young detective chided herself silently. "She's a lovely person. I hope she's not mixed up in this jinx business."

Nancy followed Professor Saunders to the large room where the mounted birds were on display. She watched him intently as he unlocked the cabinet with the empty perch and put the stuffed wryneck on its little stand. He locked the cabinet again.

Nancy noticed that the lock was the kind which could not be opened with a skeleton key. This fact made the removal of the wryneck even more puzzling.

As the man turned from the cabinet, a bell rang. He paused and Nancy knew it was his signal to go to a class. She thanked him and said good-by.

"I think I'll go home by way of the proposed site for the High Rise project," Nancy decided as she drove off. She skirted the Thurston property and parked along a dirt road next to a large open field some distance back of the bird cages. Nancy locked her car and started walking across the field.

Presently she noticed a couple standing about a hundred yards away, talking. As she drew closer Nancy thought, "That's Kammy!"

Wondering why the Eurasian girl was out here and who the man was, Nancy hastened toward them. Suddenly Kammy's companion turned. He and Nancy looked squarely at each other.

"He's the man who cut one of Mr. Thurston's cages!" Nancy murmured.

She started to run after him. At the same instant the suspect took off at a right angle toward the road. Within a few seconds he came to a car, jumped in, and sped across the field. Nancy tried to see the license number, but the car was too far away.

All this time Kammy had stood still, looking puzzled. As Nancy ran up to her, the young detective cried out, "Who was that man?"

"I don't know. I never saw him before," Kammy replied.

"Did he say why he was here?" Nancy queried.

"No, he didn't."

Kammy went on to explain that the man had told her he was a stranger in town and had asked her for directions to River Heights. "I told him I didn't know."

"Was he here when you arrived?"

"Yes, he was," Kammy said. "He was walking back from over there." Kammy pointed toward the middle of the field.

Nancy looked down and could distinctly see footprints going and returning from some spot. She decided to follow them. Kammy joined her.

Nancy was thinking, "Maybe I'll pick up a clue to his identity or why he was here." To Kammy she said, "Were you here looking over the site for the housing development?"

"Not really," Kammy replied. "I just wanted to take a stroll."

They continued to follow the footprints for

some distance and Nancy became more and more curious. She realized that not far ahead was the Thurston farmhouse.

An idea came to her. "Maybe that wire cutter was going to try it again. Then he saw Kammy coming and didn't dare go on."

Kammy kept looking at Nancy curiously and finally said, "I would like to know what you are doing. Do you expect to learn something about the stranger?"

"I hope to," Nancy answered.

The trail of footprints led the girls to a circular pit. It had been dug recently, but dirt had been shoveled back into it.

Nancy stopped and motioned to Kammy to keep from stepping closer. She had noticed there were no footprints beyond the pit. Had the stranger hidden something here? Or was he making some kind of a soil test? She quickly ruled out the latter idea, deciding that the digger would not have needed to dig up so much earth nor would he have bothered to return it to the same spot.

"Nancy, what are you thinking?" Kammy asked. "You certainly are mysterious."

The young detective smiled at her companion. "I suppose I am and I'll admit being suspicious of that stranger's reason for being here."

She began to search for a large stone. After

finding one, she told Kammy to stand back out of the way.

"I'm going to throw this," she said.

Nancy heaved it directly into the pit. Seconds later there was a terrific explosion. Dirt and stones flew in all directions!

CHAPTER V

A Criminal's Identity

KAMMY was knocked flat by the force of the explosion. None of the flying debris hit her but she lay frozen on the ground, afraid to get up. Nancy too had been bowled over but immediately arose and went to Kammy.

"Are you hurt?" she asked.

"No—no," the other girl insisted. Nancy helped Kammy to her feet. "Nancy, please tell me what's going on. How did you know an explosive had been planted here?"

Nancy said she had not known, but she became suspicious because of the newly dug area.

"Kammy, you remember the wire cutter who tried to release the birds from one of Mr. Thurston's cages?"

"Yes. Do you mean this was the same man?"

"I'm afraid so," Nancy replied. "Kammy, are you quite sure you never saw this man before and have no idea who he is?"

Again Kammy insisted she had never seen him until that day but she recalled a question that he had asked her. "He wanted to know if this was part of Mr. Thurston's property. I told him I thought it was."

Nancy was inclined to think that the stranger might be one of a group of people trying to harm the Thurstons by pretending to jinx them. The farmer sooner or later would be walking or driving over this field!

"Oh, Nancy, I am so sorry," Kammy cried. "Somehow, I feel as if I must be responsible, perhaps because of my pet Petra. But I have never tried to jinx anyone. I have always said I hope Mr. Thurston will not lose his zoo and aviary."

"Kammy," Nancy said in a sympathetic tone, "I believe you. Will you promise to phone me if you see or hear anything suspicious at the university museum or at the Thurstons'? And tell Oscar about the land mine."

"I certainly will," Kammy agreed and gave a quick smile.

The two girls walked to Nancy's car, then said good-by. As Nancy pulled away she decided that the explosion should be reported to the police, and drove directly to Harper headquarters. Nancy had heard River Heights Chief McGinnis speak of the head of the Harper department, Chief Pepper, as being a good friend.

Fortunately he was at his desk and she introduced herself. He arose and shook hands heartily.

"I'm certainly glad to meet you," he said. "McGinnis has told me so much about your expert detective work that I have the greatest admiration for you."

Nancy blushed. "I'm afraid Chief McGinnis has exaggerated."

The chief smiled at her warmly. "Miss Drew, suppose you tell me why you came to see me."

Nancy told him about the explosion in the Thurston field. "I believe the land mine was planted by the same stranger who cut a hole in one of the large bird cages."

Chief Pepper frowned. "This is very serious," he commented. "Will you please tell your story again into this tape recorder?"

Nancy repeated it, giving every detail she could remember, including the fact that the stranger had asked Kammy for directions to River Heights.

"Someone stole a wryneck from the university museum here," she went on, "and it was left on our lawn in River Heights."

"What do you think was the reason?" the chief asked her.

"My father and I are convinced that one or more persons are trying to jinx us as well as the Thurstons, probably because my father is helping Mr. Thurston on a case against the High Rise Construction Company, which wants to destroy the zoo and aviary. I also believe someone knows about Mrs. Thurston's superstitious nature and is hoping she will talk her husband into selling the farm."

As Nancy stopped dictating, the chief remarked, "That would be a great loss to the town of Harper."

After he had alerted his men to investigate the area where the land mine had been planted, Nancy said to him, "It's possible someone connected with the High Rise company buried it."

The chief looked startled and picked up a copy of the local paper. "Here's a picture of the officers of the company on a picnic."

The photograph was excellent. "And here are the workers. Suppose you study them and see if the man you saw is shown here."

Chief Pepper handed the newspaper to Nancy. "If you don't find the right one among those pictures, look through our books of photographs of lawbreakers arrested here. Some of them have been released. The books are on that shelf along the wall." He indicated them.

The police chief left his desk and Nancy set to work. The owner of the High Rise Construction Company was Ramsey Wright. He was not the suspect.

Nancy studied his face. "He doesn't look too pleasant," she thought, "but is he a criminal?"

The other High Rise officers looked even less like suspects. Nancy carefully looked at the pictures of the workmen. Not only was none of them the suspect, but all looked far more congenial than the company's executive. Nancy put the newspaper back on the chief's desk.

She walked over to the wall and read the classifications on the various volumes containing the photographs of prisoners arrested in Harper. Finally she chose a recent one marked:

> *Wanted Ex-convicts*
> *First arrest in Harper.*
> *Later prison sentences in other locations.*

"I guess this is as good a place as any to start," Nancy thought.

Seating herself at a side table, she opened the book and carefully scrutinized each face. After turning the many pages, the young detective had almost concluded that the suspect she hoped to capture was not in this volume, when a thought came to her.

"There's one face that seems slightly familiar," she said to herself and looked at it again.

The man was heavy-set and smooth shaven. His nose was long and might have been thinner if he had had a slighter build. His eyes fascinated Nancy. They were dark and somewhat squinty. The text gave his height as being medium.

Chief Pepper came in at that moment and asked, "Any progress?"

"Not really," Nancy replied, "but will you please do me a favor? Have you any tracing paper here and colored pencils?"

The chief smiled. "I think so. What are you up to?"

Nancy's eyes twinkled in reply. He buzzed for a policeman to bring in the paper and pencils. Nancy laid the thin sheet over the photograph before her. Carefully she drew a much slimmer version of the man. After adding a beard, she colored in reddish hair.

Satisfied with the result, Nancy placed the drawing before the chief. She explained, "As you can see, I've changed his appearance somewhat. Now he looks like the suspect."

Chief Pepper stared at the drawing, then held it up. "Nancy!" he exclaimed. "You've spotted a missing man! This is amazing! I shall have copies made at once and give one to each of my men."

Nancy was pleased with her work. "May I have a copy too and also one of the man in the book?"

"You certainly may," the chief replied. Again he pushed his buzzer and gave the order to the sergeant who answered.

The chief turned back to Nancy. "I notice, by the way, that you didn't change the size of the man's clothes, only made them look too big."

"No," Nancy explained, "because the person I

saw on the Thurstons' property was wearing clothes too large for him. If he's the wanted man, then he has lost a lot of weight."

She glanced at the name of the wanted man. It was Clyde O'Mayley, but he used the nickname of Slick Fingers O'Mayley. The suspect was on parole but had not reported to a parole officer and was once more on the wanted list.

"He's a very clever burglar," Chief Pepper remarked. "But cutting a hole in Mr. Thurston's cage and planting a land mine are not in his line."

The sergeant returned with copies of Clyde O'Mayley's photograph and the drawing, just as the chief's phone rang. Nancy decided to leave. Waving good-by to him, she took the pictures and walked out.

That evening she reported the latest happenings in the Thurston case to her father. He praised her work and said she had acted wisely.

"Our next move," he went on, "is to talk to the five councilmen and find out each one's views on High Rise's project. If any of them plan to vote in favor of letting Mr. Wright destroy Mr. Thurston's place, I'd like to know it."

After a pause Mr. Drew added, "I've concluded that since the High Rise people know I'm an attorney, Mr. Wright and the others wouldn't tell me much about their operation if I question them."

As he paused, Nancy's eyes lighted up. "How

"Nancy, you've spotted a missing man!"
the chief exclaimed.

about sending me?" she suggested. "They don't know me."

Mr. Drew shook his head. "I couldn't let you go alone. I'd prefer that you have an escort."

His daughter thought a few moments, then said, "How about Ned going with me?"

Ned Nickerson was a special friend of Nancy's who attended Emerson College in the winter and had held various summer jobs. Now he was selling insurance.

"Perfect," said Mr. Drew. "See if Ned can come here. Perhaps he could stay a few days."

Ned lived with his parents in Mapleton, a suburb of River Heights, and was staying there alone while his parents were in Europe. Nancy phoned and was pleased to find him at home.

"Hi!" he said. "I was going to call you tonight."

"How would you like to spend a few days at my house and help me do some sleuthing?"

"Great! I'm tired of cooking my own meals. I'll come right away."

"You're sure it won't interfere with your making an insurance sale?" Nancy questioned.

"No," he assured her. "I've sold enough so far to entitle me to a little vacation."

Ned arrived a few hours later. The following morning he and Nancy set off to interview one of the councilmen, Mr. Hinchcliff.

Ned had telephoned the councilman's office

and been told he had just left for the proposed new development near the Thurston farm. Nancy and Ned arrived there first and she was able to point out to him where the bird and animal display was.

"This whole area is so large," Ned remarked, "I should think they could put up all the high apartment houses they want to without destroying Mr. Thurston's buildings."

"I agree," Nancy said.

They saw a car coming across a field and walked toward it. The driver stepped out.

"Are you Mr. Hinchcliff?" Ned asked him.

"Yes. You're—? And this is—?"

"My friend Miss Drew and I'm Ned Nickerson."

Hinchcliff began to smile. "You're so young I presume you're not looking for an expensive apartment?"

"We're not thinking about apartments now," Nancy quickly put in. "We'd like to get your opinion about the type of apartment houses Mr. Wright plans to build."

"Oh, I like the very high ones," Mr. Hinchcliff replied, "and the more the better. People will be able to take their choice of north, east, south, or west exposures. Which would you favor?"

Nancy and Ned ignored the question.

"Will there be any recreational facilities?" Ned inquired.

"Oh yes," the councilman replied. "If you go to the High Rise Construction Company's office, someone can show you the interesting drawings of the plans. By the way, since you're not in a hurry for an apartment, you ought to wait for one of these. When do you plan to marry?"

CHAPTER VI

A New Worry

AT Mr. Hinchcliff's startling remark Nancy blushed deeply and Ned looked at the ground. They hastened to assure the councilman that they did not plan a wedding and were not looking for an apartment.

"Then why did you question me?" Mr. Hinchcliff asked, annoyed.

Nancy decided to be frank with the man. She said, "I'm tremendously interested in Mr. Thurston's zoo and aviary." Then, hoping to get a reaction from her listener and possibly learn some new facts, she added, "I'm glad the birds and animals aren't going to be taken away from here. It would be—"

Mr. Hinchcliff interrupted her. "But they are. No one would want an expensive apartment with a lot of smelly old bird and animal cages in their back yard!"

Nancy quickly assured the man that the development could be planned so that the tenants of the high-rise buildings would not be disturbed by the creatures on the farm.

"Do you think you know better than the architects?" Mr. Hinchcliff asked sarcastically.

Ned spoke up. "I think that was an uncalled-for remark."

Nancy went on, "This could be a very beautiful site with a cluster of high-rise apartment houses facing a man-made lake. There could also be a swimming pool, a park, and playground. On the other side of the lake would be Mr. Thurston's farm."

"And it would be educational too," Ned added.

Suddenly Mr. Hinchcliff exclaimed, "Say, did that crazy holdout Thurston make you call me?"

"No," Nancy answered quickly. "But I'd certainly hate to see his place destroyed. He has some fascinating birds. The children of Harper love to visit the zoo and aviary. Mr. Thurston spends a lot of time with them, explaining what the birds and animals are and in what parts of the world they live."

Mr. Hinchcliff started to walk toward his car. "All your pleading won't do any good. I've made up my mind to vote in favor of having the Thurston property condemned!"

Nancy and Ned concluded there was no use trying to convince the man. It was clear that he was sticking to his opinion and could not be persuaded to keep the farm as a lovely recreational park for the future tenants.

Nancy changed the subject. "Mr. Hinchcliff, yesterday when I was out here there was an explosion. Was the High Rise Construction Company testing the ground for rocks, perhaps?"

The councilman looked puzzled. "Explosion? What kind of explosion?"

"A land mine."

"Show me where it was," the man commanded.

Nancy led the way to the spot. Mr. Hinchcliff and Ned gazed in amazement at the hole in the earth.

With a frown the councilman said, "I'll find out from Mr. Wright about this."

He walked off with a worried look on his face. After stepping into his car, he put it in gear and roared away.

Ned grinned. "Friendly soul. Say, Nancy, you may have set up a little war in the council!"

Nancy laughed. "I hope it accomplishes some good," she said. "At least it may make the men suspicious of the High Rise people."

Ned asked what else she had seen at the time of the explosion. She told him about Slick Fingers O'Mayley. When she got to the part about looking through the pictures at police headquarters, he grinned and said, "You're really something, Nancy!"

"I made a drawing of a thin version of the stout parolee. Chief Pepper is sure he's the man we want, but so far none of us can figure out any motive for his planting a land mine here."

Nancy added there was no proof of any connection between Slick Fingers and men in the High Rise company.

Ned suggested that he and Nancy have lunch in Harper, then visit the Thurstons. She agreed and they drove into town. About two o'clock they set off for the zoo and aviary.

Nancy rang the front doorbell of the Thurston farmhouse. In a few moments a voice inside said, "Who's there?"

"It's Nancy Drew and a friend."

"Then come in."

Ned opened the door, and the couple crossed the hall. They found Mrs. Thurston in her wheelchair in the living room. Nancy introduced Ned, then asked how the woman was feeling.

"I'm very nervous," Mrs. Thurston replied. "Very upset, very upset indeed."

"May I ask why?" Nancy questioned.

Mrs. Thurston threw her arms up dramatically. "More bad luck has fallen on us! We've been double jinxed!"

"More trouble?" Nancy exclaimed, incredulous. "Can you tell us what happened?"

The woman began to twist a handkerchief

nervously in her hands. "Poor Oscar! Oh, why do these things happen to us?"

Nancy and Ned waited patiently for her to explain. Finally she said, "Nearly all the birds in one of the cages are ill. Oscar and Rausch are busy treating them with antibiotics but a few have already died."

"What's the matter with them?" Ned asked.

"Is Petra all right?" Nancy queried. She turned to Ned and said, "That's the name of Kammy's wryneck."

Mrs. Thurston ground her teeth. "That girl! She's been getting free board here in return for helping Oscar. Now she walks off and takes Petra with her!"

Nancy felt that she must come to Kammy's defense. "I suppose she was afraid Petra would become ill too. She not only loves that bird, Mrs. Thurston, but she considers it as her link to her native land. She declares it brings her good, not bad, luck."

Ned spoke up. "If Kammy isn't here, then your husband is short-handed for helpers."

"Yes, he is. Of course Rausch works hard, but he mostly takes care of the animals while Oscar watches all the birds."

Nancy and Ned looked at each other, then she said, "Let's go pitch in."

They excused themselves and went out the

kitchen door. Mr. Thurston was just coming to
the house. Nancy introduced Ned.

"We came to help you," she said.

"That's very kind," he said. "All the sick birds
are in the last cage. Don't go in there. They
probably have ornithosis and humans can catch
it. I'll continue with my treatment.

"If you want to help, open the door of that
shed over there and bring back pails of bird food.
All the different bags are marked. Breeds of birds
eat certain food that others don't. You'll see the
feeding troughs. When you get through with that
work, fill the large watering cans and pour the
water into the various containers inside the
cages."

Nancy said to Oscar, "It's too bad Kammy left
you. Where did she go?"

Oscar explained that she had taken a room at
the university until the birds were well again.
The man heaved a great sigh.

"I believe Kammy is on the level, but my wife
is suspicious of her. She thinks that Kammy and
Petra together have jinxed us. Of course I don't
put any stock in such nonsense, but I can't talk
Martha out of her beliefs."

He went off to attend to his sick birds. Nancy
and Ned hurried to get the feed, then they unlocked and entered one cage after another. Ned
remarked again and again how beautiful the birds
were and tried to learn the names of some of the

more exotic species from signs attached to the doors.

Presently the couple finished their work but Oscar was still busy.

"Oscar didn't say anything about our cleaning the cages but I think they need it," Ned remarked. "Let's do what we can." Nancy agreed with the young man's suggestion.

He got a long-handled scraper and Nancy took an extra stiff broom. They worked for nearly half an hour. The sun was going down and they decided to quit.

"This is a tough job," Ned remarked as they started for the main house. "Much harder than selling insurance."

Nancy laughed. "And more strenuous than solving mysteries."

Oscar joined them and the three entered the kitchen together. Suddenly they became aware of moaning sounds coming from the living room. As they rushed forward, Oscar cried out, "Martha must be in trouble!"

CHAPTER VII

Leaping Specter

OSCAR rushed toward the living room, with Nancy and Ned following. Martha Thurston was slumped forward in her wheelchair, moaning and sobbing. She rocked back and forth and wrung her hands.

"Martha dear!" her husband exclaimed. "What is the matter?"

She did not reply. Oscar put an arm around his wife and pleaded with her to tell him what had happened. She just kept on moaning and sobbing.

Nancy spoke up. "Perhaps if Ned and I go outside, she will talk to you."

Suddenly Mrs. Thurston seemed to come out of a trancelike state. She stared at the others in the room, then began to cry hysterically.

"It was awful! Awful!"

"Please tell us about it," Oscar said gently.

"Is the specter gone?" his wife asked.

The others stared at her, wondering if she had really come out of the trance. Suddenly she sat up very straight. Martha Thurston looked all around, blinked her eyes, and shook her head.

"It's gone!" she answered her own question. "I'm all right now, but Oscar, the—"

"Are you sure you weren't dreaming?" her husband asked softly.

"No, no," his wife insisted. She opened her left hand. "Here's proof. The flying specter dropped this into my lap. The symbol is a jinx!"

Mrs. Thurston held up a plain piece of paper, now quite crumpled, on which a crudely drawn circle was inscribed with one straight line running from north to south and another from east to west.

"Do you know what this is?" she asked.

Nancy spoke up. "No. It looks like a cross in a circle. Does it have a special meaning?"

"Indeed it does," Martha Thurston said. "It's a sign of bad luck. It means imprisonment, detention, an emergency trip to the hospital, or something equally as bad. Oh, Oscar, what are we going to do?"

Her husband asked, "You say this was dropped into your lap? How? By whom?"

Mrs. Thurston explained that she had been dozing in her chair because the fading light of the late afternoon had made her feel drowsy.

"I was suddenly awakened by a very bright light that shone right in front of me. It was so dazzling that I had to squint my eyes. Without warning a specter leaped from the hall all the way across this room."

"What did it look like?" Nancy asked.

"It seemed to be the figure of a thin, tall man but his face, if he had one, was covered with white veils and he had on a long, flowing white robe. Suddenly the figure leaped back toward the hall. On the way he dropped this piece of paper in my lap."

"Where did the specter go?" Ned asked.

"When he reached the hall," Mrs. Thurston replied, "the light disappeared and so did he. I don't know whether he was a ghost or not."

The woman closed her eyes as if to blot out the sight. "Maybe he went out the door but I didn't hear it open or close. Perhaps he vanished through the wall!"

Oscar patted his wife's shoulder. "Try to forget the whole thing, my dear. It's time for your medication." He winked at Nancy and Ned.

At once Nancy asked if she might prepare some tea and toast for Mrs. Thurston and the man nodded. "And, Oscar, when you're ready," Nancy went on, "I'll be glad to fix your supper."

Mr. Thurston turned to his wife. "Do you hear that?" he asked. "Wouldn't you like Nancy and Ned to stay and have supper with us?"

His wife's whole attitude changed. She smiled and said, "I'm sorry I acted so badly. Your staying would be delightful, but it's too bad to put you to so much trouble."

Nancy chuckled. "I don't mind. And thank you for the invitation. I'll call home and say we're having supper here."

Nancy was glad to have the excuse to stay for another reason. She wanted to hunt around for clues to the specter. While she and Ned were in the kitchen, they discussed the strange incident.

"I hate to say this," Ned remarked, "but Mrs. Thurston could have made that circle with the lines herself and then had a dream about the specter."

Nancy considered the possibility, but said she was inclined to think the incident had really happened. "The front door was unlocked and anyone could easily come in," she added. "Knowing that Mrs. Thurston was alone in the house, the specter took advantage of a good chance to pull his spooky trick."

Ned remarked that he thought Oscar was the most patient man he had ever met. Nancy nodded and told him Bess's theory that part of Mrs. Thurston's poor health was due to fear, induced by her superstitions.

"She's probably right."

Oscar came into the kitchen as Ned said this and told the young people that his wife was now lying on the couch. She seemed quite composed and would likely fall asleep.

"Nancy," he said, "do you think you could fix supper for us by yourself?"

"Certainly. Is there a special dish you'd like to have?"

Oscar said he was not fussy. "Anything will do and don't go to any trouble." He added that he wanted to check on the birds again.

"I might need a little help. Ned, would you be willing to go with me?"

"Glad to."

The two men went outside. Nancy hunted for the telephone. Finding it, she called Hannah Gruen to tell her where she and Ned were and that they were staying to supper.

"I'm the cook!" she said, laughing. "Too bad you aren't here. The meal would be so much better."

Hannah chuckled. "You do very well, Nancy. But don't try any fancy dishes on strangers. Nothing with a French name. Just good old American food."

After acquainting herself with the contents of the refrigerator, Nancy decided on the menu. It would include split pea soup, broiled lamb chops, mashed potatoes and creamed spinach.

"But what about dessert?" she asked herself, seeing nothing in the refrigerator, freezer, or on the kitchen counters. She opened a cabinet door and discovered several cans of fruit.

"I'll make boiled custard and after it's chilled I'll pour it over canned peaches," she decided.

Nancy became so engrossed in cooking, she did not notice how time was slipping away. First she made the custard, and while it was cooling, went into the dining room to set the table. Everything seemed to take much longer than usual because she did not know where certain dishes and silverware were kept.

"This is kind of a mystery game in itself," she said to herself.

Finally the table was ready and she went back to the kitchen. The potatoes were soft enough to be mashed, so she put on the soup to heat and cooked the frozen spinach.

Next she lighted the broiler, then checked the wall clock. "Oscar and Ned have been gone a long time," she thought. "Oh, I hope this doesn't mean more birds are sick!"

Nancy went in to the living room to peek at Mrs. Thurston, who was sound asleep, and returned to the kitchen window. There was no sign of the two men.

"I'm certainly not going to broil the chops until Ned and Oscar come in," she determined.

Another five minutes went by. "I'll walk outside and see where they are!" Nancy decided.

She turned off all the burners and the broiler, then went to lock the front door. She left the house by the kitchen door and locked that too. Pocketing the key, she hurried toward the first set of cages.

At first she could see nothing unusual, but the young sleuth suddenly detected a peculiar odor in the air.

"It smells like chloroform," she thought.

Nancy hurried on. As she neared the cage containing the sick birds, she stopped short and gasped. Sprawled on the ground not far from these helpless creatures were Oscar and Ned, unconscious!

CHAPTER VIII

Unseen Visitor

TERRIFIED about the condition of Ned and Oscar, Nancy rushed toward them. The peculiar sweetish odor she detected grew stronger as she moved closer.

"I'd better cover my nose and mouth," Nancy thought.

She whipped off her scarf, and tied it securely over her face just below her eyes. Then she hurried to Ned's side. His weight seemed to have doubled. With difficulty she dragged him away from the overpowering smell. Then she rushed back and pulled Oscar by his shoulders over to where Ned lay. She felt their pulses and found they were normal.

"Thank goodness," Nancy murmured.

At this moment a cool breeze sprang up that Nancy hoped would soon restore the two men to consciousness.

"The birds!" she thought suddenly, and hurried back to the cage of sick ones. To her horror they all lay on the ground, their feet in the air.

"They're dead!" Nancy murmured. "How terrible!"

She wondered if they had died from the disease or if the intruder had deliberately sprayed them with the killing substance. With these questions burning in her mind, the young detective hurried back to Oscar and Ned. They were still unconscious.

Nancy was alarmed that they showed no signs of recovery. "I hate to tell Mrs. Thurston. She'll be so worried about Oscar it may have a bad effect on her health."

As Nancy was debating what to do, she removed the scarf from her face. To her relief, Ned slowly opened his eyes. He looked at her, then closed them again.

Nancy knelt by his side. "Ned, are you all right?" she asked.

Once more he opened his eyes, then said weakly, "Where am I?"

"You're in a safe place," Nancy assured him. "Just take it easy."

Her words aroused Oscar, who blinked several times, then finally opened his eyes wide.

"Who are you?" he asked, looking at Nancy. "I can't see very well. Everything is blurry."

Again Nancy was terrified. Had the numbing

substance affected the man's eyesight permanently?

"As soon as you feel like walking, we'll go into the house and bathe your eyes," she said gently.

A few minutes later both he and Ned declared they felt all right, although Ned still looked groggy as he got to his feet.

Nancy stood between them and linked arms with them. She guided the two to the kitchen, where they sat down at once.

"Oscar, tell me where your eye lotion is, and I'll get it," Nancy offered.

The man said it was on the second floor in a bathroom cabinet. She went for it and as soon as she returned filled an eye cup with the fluid. After Oscar had bathed his eyes several times, he declared they were much better.

"How's Martha?" he inquired.

Nancy said she had been resting quietly. "I decided not to tell her what happened to you two."

"That is best," Oscar agreed. He smiled wanly. "We'll keep that as our little secret."

Nancy told him and Ned that most of the dinner was ready but she had to broil the lamb chops. "Do you feel like eating now?"

"I do," Ned said quickly, and Oscar nodded.

As Nancy turned on the stove burners again, she asked the men to tell her what had happened.

"I was going into the cage with the sick birds,"

Oscar said, "and told Ned to stay outside. Before I had a chance to open the gate, somebody crept up from behind, put his arms around Ned's and my necks, and held pieces of cotton saturated with some sweet-smelling stuff right over our faces. One good whiff and we were goners."

Nancy suggested that perhaps they could find the discarded pieces of cotton to determine what the knockout fluid had been. All this time she had said nothing about the dead birds. But now Nancy felt she should, in case Oscar wanted to do something about them.

When he heard the sad story, Oscar lowered his head and sighed. "What's done is done," he said philosophically. "But it is a great loss to me, not only for sentimental reasons, but this is my livelihood. I can almost agree with Martha that we have been jinxed."

Ned tried to console the bird owner by telling him that the man who had accosted them would certainly be caught and made to pay restitution.

"I hope so—and soon," Oscar said.

In the meantime Nancy set the piping hot food on the table. Mr. Thurston had little appetite and had to be coaxed to eat something. To please his wife who had awakened and joined them at the table, he bravely sampled all the courses.

As soon as they finished eating, Martha asked

Oscar to carry her to bed. While the couple was upstairs, Nancy and Ned cleared the table and washed and dried the dishes. Nancy had just finished cleaning the broiler when Oscar came downstairs.

"I want to go outside and look around," he said. "Nancy and Ned, will you come along? Let's see if we can pick up any clues to the unseen intruder."

Nancy and Oscar got flashlights. While the man went to the rest of the cages to be sure none of the other still-healthy species had been harmed, Nancy and Ned began to search for unfamiliar or freshly-made footprints. An intense hunt revealed only that there were so many of them it would be difficult to distinguish a stranger's from those of friendly callers.

Nancy had a hunch that the person who had attacked Oscar and Ned would not have gone near the house. For this reason she followed several sets of footprints that led in a direction away from the dwelling and toward the road.

She and Ned found a few separate prints in a muddy area, but they were only partially clear because the man who had made them had been running and skidding in the softened ground.

"I guess we'll have to give up," Ned suggested.

At the road the couple turned and started back. They had gone about halfway to the cages, with

Nancy flashing her light from left to right, when suddenly she stopped.

"See something?" Ned asked.

Nancy went over to a clump of bushes and stared down at an empty can with a new label on it.

Chloroform!

"I guess this was what the intruder used," she said.

Ned started to pick it up, but Nancy caught his arm. "Let's wrap this up so we won't ruin any fingerprints on it," she suggested.

She removed her scarf and carefully tied it around the can. Ned carried it back to the house. Oscar came to the kitchen and they showed it to him.

"I think," said Nancy, "that what happened today should be reported to the police. Suppose Ned and I take this evidence to Chief Pepper and tell him the story."

"That's a good idea," Oscar agreed.

A little while later she and Ned said good-by and told the bird owner they certainly hoped he would have no more trouble.

He smiled at the couple. "You are wonderful," he said. "However, I can't hope for good luck yet. But maybe there'll be a break soon. Nancy, I'm depending on you and your father to straighten out this whole problem."

Ned grinned. "The Drews will do it!" he assured the man.

Half an hour later he and Nancy arrived at police headquarters in Harper. Chief Pepper was just going off duty, but he waited to talk to them. Nancy introduced Ned, and the officer led the couple into his office.

Nancy told him that there had been sabotage at the Thurston place. "Ned will explain what happened to him and Oscar."

As the chief listened to the story he frowned again and again.

Finally he said, "This is serious. If things get any worse, I believe we'll have to post a guard out there to spot intruders."

Nancy now handed the chief the scarf with its contents. "I surmise that the can has fingerprints on it. That's why I didn't touch it."

Chief Pepper smiled. "You're a true detective, all right." He opened his desk drawer and took out a cellophane bag into which he rolled the can. "I'll send this to our laboratory at once."

The officer promised to let Nancy know the results as well as Oscar Thurston. Then the young people said good-by and went to their car.

As they were driving slowly through the main street of Harper, Nancy suddenly said, "Ned, would you be willing to go with me to the ballet?"

"Where?"

"Right here. I saw a sign back there. We just have enough time to catch the evening performance and I think maybe we can pick up a clue there."

"A clue at the ballet?" Ned asked, puzzled.

"Yes," Nancy replied. "And maybe a very good one."

CHAPTER IX

The Puzzling Circle

CHUCKLING, Ned took his eyes off the street just long enough to glance at Nancy seated beside him in his car.

"You certainly can jump from one clue to another pretty fast. So you're not going to tell me what your latest hunch is?"

Nancy laughed. "No, I'm not. This one you'll have to figure out yourself," she teased.

"Okay. I'll find a place to park and we'll go into the ballet."

The performance was about to begin as the couple took their seats. The program was drawn from a broad range of traditional to contemporary dances.

The first selection was set in a woodland scene. Four dancers in filmy pale-gray costumes flitted across stage. Nancy glanced at Ned as he shifted uncomfortably. She could see that he was not particularly interested.

"He'll like the next number better," she thought.

The lithe dancers had barely left the stage when several male dancers, dressed in green frogmen costumes, entered. While Nancy was intrigued by the idea of dancing in flipper-like footgear, Ned wanted to laugh at first. Not wishing to embarrass his companion, he merely grinned. After a while he admitted to himself that the costumes, particularly the undersea headgear, were clever. Even the dance which combined familiar movements with swimlike steps began to fascinate him.

When the number ended, Ned turned to Nancy. "I think I have a clue to your clue. You think one of these leaping frogmen might be the specter who frightened Mrs. Thurston."

Nancy merely smiled. Ned's surmise was correct, but none of the dancers had shown the talent to leap the distance that Mrs. Thurston had indicated. During the intermission she told Ned she would like to talk to the stage manager or director of the troupe.

The couple went to the lobby and spoke to the woman in the box office. Ned made the request of her and gave their names.

"I'll see," she said and disappeared into a rear office. The woman soon returned and smilingly announced, "Mr. Van Camp will see you after the show. He'll be backstage with the dancers."

While waiting for the second part of the ballet to start, Nancy began to formulate questions to ask the man. Soon the houselights dimmed and the curtains rolled back.

The third number was a solo and so interesting to Nancy that she sat on the edge of her seat and watched intently. The dancer was a star performer named Boris Borovsky. His muscular control and grace, combined with a handsome appearance, were captivating. He interspersed the dance with spectacular leaps. During one dramatic movement Boris swooped through the air from one end of the stage to the other with such ease he really seemed to be flying. Nancy overheard a comment that perhaps Boris was Peter Pan in disguise.

Ned was fascinated too. When the number was over, he whispered to Nancy, "Is he your villain?"

She shrugged. "We'll find out after the show."

The applause was thunderous and continued until Borovsky began to dance an encore. Other numbers followed, but none could equal his, which had been the high point of the evening.

When the curtains were drawn finally, Nancy and Ned walked toward the stage and opened a side door. They ascended a few steps and watched the scene onstage. A man in a business suit, apparently the director, was talking to the dancers, who were still in costume.

Nancy and Ned politely waited until he had

dismissed the ensemble. Then, as the man turned to leave, they stepped onto the stage.

"Mr. Van Camp?" Ned asked.

The man nodded. "You are the couple who asked to see me?"

"Yes," Nancy replied. "First, I want to tell you how much I enjoyed the entire ballet. Your dancers and the selections were really wonderful."

Ned smiled. "I admit Nancy dragged me here, but I found myself liking the performance very much—particularly the high jumper."

The director smiled at Ned's athletic reference to the troupe's star dancer, and Nancy was grateful for an opening to ask her first question. "Mr. Van Camp, do you know of any other male dancer in this area who can compare with Boris Borovsky?"

"Yes, I do," the director replied. "He used to be with this troupe and I hated to lose him. He was one of the best talents I ever worked with. Unfortunately I had to let him go."

Mr. Van Camp looked questioningly at the young people. "Did you have a particular reason for wanting to know?"

Nancy wondered just how much she should reveal and replied, "Yes. My father is an attorney and something strange happened on the case he's handling. A clue to someone involved might be a male dancer who can leap unusually high."

Mr. Van Camp now divulged the fact that he

had discharged the other dancer for his disreputable connections and unprofessional attitude.

"I don't know what he's doing now, but I imagine he's been dodging the law since he left here. His real name is Mervin Gantry but the stage name he uses is Merv Marvel."

Ned asked, "Could this Merv Marvel guy be mixed up in any kind of a land deal?"

Mr. Van Camp frowned. "I imagine he could be mixed up in almost anything. Merv had a strange way of mesmerizing people. He could get them to do just about anything."

Nancy was struck by the word mesmerized. "How did he *mesmerize* people?"

The director said he had even heard a rumor that Marvel had tried fleecing superstitious people by scaring them with signs of warning and strange omens of bad luck.

"What kind of signs?" Nancy asked quickly.

"Various kinds, I was told," the director replied. "By the way, if you ever come across him don't let him try to sell you anything!"

"Thanks for the tip," Ned replied with a grin.

"Could you tell me," Nancy persisted, "what any of the signs were?"

Mr. Van Camp said that Merv was very angry at being discharged. "He left one of his symbols on my desk."

The director pulled a note pad from his pocket and with a pencil drew a circle with a cross inside. Nancy wanted to shout for joy, but restrained herself as did Ned who said nothing. She had picked up a real clue!

Mr. Van Camp went on, "I've been told that this symbol means bad luck of some sort."

Nancy did not comment but wondered, "Is this a private mark the ex-dancer uses or is he a member of some witchcraft group?"

Out of the corners of their eyes, the couple became aware of some dancers still waiting in the wings to talk to Mr. Van Camp. Nancy and Ned started to thank him and excuse themselves when he surprised them by asking:

"Have you people ever danced ballet?"

Ned laughed. "Only around a football field."

Nancy told him that she had taken ballet lessons and loved them. "Sometime I'd like to learn to leap," she said. "We only studied it a little in acrobatic class."

Mr. Van Camp's eyes twinkled. He called out, "Boris, come over here!"

The agile dancer walked forward and was introduced to Nancy and Ned.

Mr. Van Camp repeated Nancy's remark to Boris, who smiled. "I'd be happy to help her, but first let me see you dance a little, Nancy."

"Music!" Mr. Van Camp called out to the musicians who were in conference with their conductor.

Nancy was flushed with excitement. She took off her shoes. As soon as the music started she found it easy to execute simple movements, then with increasing confidence, more complicated ones. Some of the professional dancers came on stage and applauded.

"You are excellent," Boris complimented Nancy. "Take my hand."

As they started to dance together, Ned was amazed by his friend's obvious talent. He began to clap too.

Boris himself seemed pleased with his pupil. As the tempo of the music increased, the star's performance encouraged Nancy to make more strenuous leaps. Though Nancy could feel a twinge of muscle cramp, she was determined to dance her best.

When the music ended, Boris surprised and embarrassed Nancy by giving her a hug and a kiss and saying, "You're wonderful!"

Nancy was pleased, but decided she would always prefer Ned as her steady dancing partner. She thanked Boris Borovsky and wished him continued luck in his career. Mr. Van Camp came to pat her on the shoulder. "Any time you're looking for extra work, let me know," he said, smiling. "It has been a real pleasure meeting you and Ned. I certainly hope our paths cross again."

"I hope so too," Nancy replied. Lowering her voice, she added, "And thank you for the information about Merv Marvel. I'll pass it along to my father."

Blushing happily, she left the theater with Ned. He was very quiet and she wondered if he was embarrassed by her ballet exhibition, or was he sulking a bit out of jealousy?

She herself said little, but at the Drew home, she began to relate the full story of the day's happenings to her father and Hannah Gruen. She had hardly begun to speak when Ned arose.

"If you don't mind," he said, "I think I'll go to bed. I'm really beat." He said good night and went upstairs.

"Ned doesn't seem like himself," Mr. Drew remarked. "Nancy, did something happen between you two today?"

Nancy explained about Ned's and Mr. Thurston's unpleasant experience.

"Then no doubt Ned is feeling the aftermath of it all. Sleep is the best thing for him."

Her father's comment caused Nancy to wonder if she had been inconsiderate of Ned in suggesting they attend the ballet. She chided herself for it, then went on with her detailed report. Nearly an hour passed before they went upstairs. The lawyer praised his daughter for having uncovered the clue to the leaping specter.

Ned, amazed, began to clap for Nancy.

"I'll have someone start working on that angle at once," he said.

Nancy found that she too was very tired and dropped off to sleep at once. It was some time in the early morning that she was awakened by voices out in the hall.

Peering from her door, she observed Hannah and her father talking together worriedly and she asked what was troubling them.

"Ned is very ill," her father said.

CHAPTER X

Unpleasant Councilman

"NED ill?" Nancy repeated. "I must go in and see him!"

Mr. Drew put a firm hand on his daughter's shoulder and shook his head. "We don't know what the trouble is yet and it may be contagious. What you can do is telephone Dr. Black and ask him if he can come over at once."

She disliked the idea of waking the physician so early, but realized her father would not have made the request unless it was an emergency. In a few seconds Nancy was speaking with Dr. Black.

"This is Nancy Drew, Dr. Black. My friend Ned Nickerson is visiting us. He has suddenly become very ill. Would it be possible for you to come right over so that we'll know what to do?"

"I'll be there in a little while," the physician replied.

After he arrived, Nancy and Hannah waited

downstairs. The housekeeper said suddenly, "Ned might have food poisoning. I've tried to serve only wholesome meals. But maybe my—"

Nancy interrupted to assure her that her cooking was not the cause of Ned's illness. All of them had eaten the same food and none of the others had become ill. She wondered, however, if some of the supper she had prepared at the Thurstons had been spoiled. Nancy dismissed the thought upon recalling that she had shared the identical meal.

When she told this to Hannah, the housekeeper said, "Then all I can conclude is that, even though I'm not superstitious, Ned must have been jinxed at the Thurston farm."

Her remark startled Nancy. She went to the telephone to find out how Oscar was feeling after the attack upon him and Ned. He answered the phone at once and assured Nancy that he felt quite well. "Evidently I suffered no ill effects from what happened yesterday. I'm about to go out and work with the birds."

Nancy said good-by. "What can be the matter with Ned?" she asked herself.

Just then the door to Ned's room opened. Mr. Drew came out, followed by Dr. Black. As they reached the foot of the stairs, Nancy asked, "Please tell me about Ned. How is he?"

While patting her on the shoulder, the physician answered, "He's a pretty sick boy, Nancy, but I believe I know what's causing the trouble and with correct treatment he'll improve quickly."

Dr. Black went on to say that he suspected Ned was suffering from an attack of ornithosis, a disease which is carried by sick birds. "I understand from your father that Ned's been in contact with some at the Thurston farm. I'm having tests made at the lab and I'll let you know."

Instantly Nancy offered to play nurse for Ned. The doctor shook his head. "If it is ornithosis, it's quite contagious. All of you might easily catch it. I shall see about having Ned removed to a hospital."

Hannah Gruen stepped forward. "Please don't do that. I'll put on a surgeon's mask and take care of Ned myself."

"Where are Ned's parents?" Dr. Black asked.

"In Europe," Nancy replied. "Oh, Dad, please let Ned stay here."

Mr. Drew smiled but said emphatically, "We'll have Dr. Black decide that."

"I'll let you know," the physician replied.

He left the house, carrying his doctor's kit. Nancy turned to her father. "Dad, you've been exposed to Ned. I hope you don't get sick!"

The tall, handsome lawyer grinned. "I'm in tiptop shape, Nancy," he said, thumping his chest. He put an arm around his daughter. "Please stop worrying."

This was not easy for Nancy to do. She said nothing more, however, and went into the kitchen to help Hannah prepare breakfast.

During the meal, Mr. Drew and Hannah took turns going upstairs to peek at Ned. They reported that he was asleep.

When the telephone rang, Nancy hastened to answer it. Dr. Black was calling with his report.

"Your friend Ned definitely has ornithosis," he stated. "I will have medication sent over at once. It's an antibiotic which should alleviate the virus immediately. Nancy, I think you should inform the Thurstons about Ned's symptoms."

"I'll give him a ring at once and tell him," Nancy promised.

She put in a second call to the farm. To her relief Mr. Thurston told her he had already disposed of the lifeless birds and thoroughly sprayed the cages with disinfectant.

"Fortunately none of the other birds have been affected," he said, "and Rausch reports that all the animals in the zoo are okay."

Nancy felt relieved. "Oh I'm glad."

After hearing about Ned's condition, Oscar told her to give the young man his best wishes. "Tell him how sorry I am he picked up the virus at my bird farm. I'm wondering," he went on, "if by any chance the intruder deliberately infected the birds in order to make us believe we're jinxed."

"That's a possibility," Nancy remarked. "In

any case, it's a shame you had to lose all those beautiful birds."

Nancy said she assumed it would be safe now for her, Bess, and George to help with the cleaning and feeding of the healthy birds. Oscar gladly accepted her offer. As soon as Nancy finished talking to him, she called Bess, then George. Both were astounded to hear her report about Ned.

"Since I'm not allowed to help take care of him," said Nancy, "how about the three of us pitching in at the Thurston farm?"

The cousins eagerly agreed to go. On the way, the girls decided to buy some groceries and prepare a couple of meals for the Thurstons.

When they arrived at the farm, they again found Martha Thurston in her wheelchair. After a quick pleasant greeting, the woman began to relate a terrible dream about a giant bulldozer coming on their property, knocking over all the buildings, and letting the birds fly away.

"You were overtired yesterday," Nancy said to her kindly. "That's why you dreamed last night. Try to forget the whole thing. We'll show you what we brought, then we'll go out to the cages and help your husband."

The woman was very much pleased with the gift of meats and vegetables and an angel cake. The visitors put the articles away, then headed for the back yard.

When the work was finished, Oscar said, "You

three are certainly good workers. Thank you."

While Bess and George prepared lunch, Nancy told Oscar about the conversation with Mr. Hinchcliff. The bird owner was disappointed by the man's attitude but said he still hoped the town council would vote in his favor.

"You know other farms are involved in various developments of Mr. Wright's, but none has a setup like mine."

"I'm going to call on Councilman Ryan this afternoon," Nancy told him. "He owns the clothing store, doesn't he?"

"Yes, he does."

Oscar gazed into the distance before speaking again. Finally he said, "I hope you won't find Mr. Ryan difficult."

"Is he supposed to be?" Nancy asked, smiling.

The man nodded. "He's a great bargainer and in the town council meetings never budges from his original opinion. Nancy, I wish you luck. Actually I believe you can handle him." Oscar chuckled.

About two-thirty the three girls set off. When they reached the shopping center in Harper, they parked in front of the clothing store and went inside. Nancy asked for the proprietor and was told he was in his office on the balcony.

"I guess it's all right for you to go up," said the young man who had answered her query. "Just knock."

Nancy, Bess, and George ascended the stairway, with Nancy in the lead. She knocked on a door marked Mr. Ryan. A loud dictatorial voice boomed, "Come in!"

As the three callers walked in, Mr. Ryan, who was seated behind his desk, greeted them with a snappy question.

"Do you all work here?"

"No, we don't," Nancy told him.

When he made no attempt to carry on a conversation, she said, "We heard about High Rise's new development plans. I suppose it will bring a lot of new shoppers into town and that will please you."

"I suppose it will," he said evenly. "Are you thinking of applying for jobs in my store when the development opens?"

The girls were a bit amused by his assumption but kept straight faces. Nancy said, "Wouldn't we be a little early to think of that?"

"Yes, you would be. Well, what did you come for? I can't give you much of my time. I'm a very busy man."

Bess assured Mr. Ryan they would not stay long. She turned to Nancy, "Tell him what you have in mind."

"Mr. Ryan," said Nancy, "we've been looking over the area where the apartment buildings may be put. We understand that these will replace Mr. Thurston's zoo and aviary."

"That's right," the shop owner agreed.

"Have you ever thought," Nancy asked, "how much more attractive the development would be if the Thurston farm were left intact?"

Mr. Ryan gave a start. "What do you mean?"

Nancy told him that she could visualize the development very clearly. A cluster of high-rise apartment houses would face on a man-made lake. There would be a swimming pool, a park, and a playground. And on the other side of the lake Mr. Thurston's zoo and aviary as an added attraction.

"The tenants' children would love to go over there and see the birds and animals and hear Oscar Thurston talk about them. It would be very educational and relaxing for adults too."

The shop owner thought this over a few seconds, then suddenly a sneering look came over his face. "Who sent you here to propose this to me?"

"Nobody," Nancy replied. George and Bess echoed the comment.

"I don't believe you," Mr. Ryan shouted. "Well," the councilman added, "I don't care who it was and you tell him for me to mind his own business! I'll vote exactly the way I want to without any advice from someone else! I've already made up my mind that the Thurston farm must go!"

He arose from his desk chair and walked to the door. Opening it wide, he glared at the callers and said, "You've already taken up too much of my valuable time. I would appreciate your leaving at once!"

The three girls walked out of the office without saying a word. Then George burst out, "What a mean man he is!"

Bess added, "I never met anybody so narrow-minded and pigheaded in all my life!"

Nancy heaved a great sigh. "That certainly was a disappointing interview, but I'm not giving up. I'll call on the other councilmen as soon as I have a chance." She added that there were three more.

When the girls reached the car, Nancy asked George to drive.

"I don't know why, but I'm really exhausted. I'll take the car from your house."

George dropped her cousin Bess at the Marvin home, then went to her own house. She said good-by to Nancy and advised her to take a nap or at least to go to bed early that evening.

"Will do," Nancy replied and drove off.

After putting her car in the garage, she entered the house through the kitchen door. Hannah Gruen came bustling down the front stairway into the hall to meet her.

"Oh, Nancy," the housekeeper cried, "Ned seems to be much worse. I can't reach either the doctor or your father on the phone. I don't know what to do!"

She went on, "Ned is slightly delirious and he keeps calling for you, insisting he must see you. I don't know what to do!"

Instantly Nancy rushed to the stairway. "If Ned wants to see me, he's going to!"

Hannah Gruen grabbed the girl's arm. "Dr. Black and your father told you not to go in that room."

"I know," Nancy replied sheepishly. "I'll stop at the door and call to Ned."

The housekeeper released the girl's arm and Nancy raced up the steps, two at a time. "Oh, Ned," she kept saying to herself, "you must get better!"

CHAPTER XI

Missing Pet

NANCY stood at the doorway of Ned's bedroom. He was tossing restlessly and calling Nancy's name over and over. Now and then he would mumble something she could not understand.

"I must find out what it is he's trying to tell me," she thought, and moved closer to the bed.

The patient opened his eyes partway and realized that Nancy was standing beside him. He put out a hand as if to grasp hers. It was all she could do to restrain herself from taking his. She pretended not to see it and he dropped his hand listlessly back on the bed.

"Ned," she said soothingly, "everything's going to be all right. Do you want to tell me what's troubling you?"

"Yes," he mumbled. "Slick Fingers probably has this. Find him, Nancy." Ned closed his eyes and fell into a deep sleep.

Nancy stood pondering Ned's startling statement. What had he meant? After a few moments' thought, she decided that he figured Slick Fingers had contracted ornithosis from the diseased birds at the Thurston aviary.

"Ned thinks he must be lying ill somewhere and probably had a doctor. If I can only locate Slick Fingers through a hospital or a doctor, the authorities can arrest him."

The question was how far away from River Heights the parolee might be. Was he still in the area of Harper? Nancy concluded that this was likely since Slick Fingers was working against the Thurstons.

Nancy glanced at her watch. It was still early afternoon.

"I'll drive over to Harper and inquire at the hospitals there if a Clyde O'Mayley is a patient."

She told Hannah Gruen her plan and said she would return as soon as possible.

"It seems to me," the housekeeper remarked, "that your errand is like hunting for a needle in a haystack."

Nancy smiled. "Why, Hannah dear, you've always told me that if you have the right magnet you can find even a needle in a haystack."

Mrs. Gruen laughed heartily. "I'm glad you remembered some of my teaching."

Nancy hugged her. "You have no idea how much you've really helped me in my detective work. Well, let's hope I find the needle which, in this case, is Slick Fingers."

"Watch your step!" Hannah warned.

Nancy nodded and began to check a telephone directory for the Harper hospitals. There were two: General and Mercy.

In a few minutes Nancy was rolling along the highway in her convertible. After entering Harper, she drove directly to General Hospital. To her disappointment, she learned that Clyde O'Mayley was not a patient nor had he visited the clinic for medical assistance.

"But I've just started my search," the young detective consoled herself. "I'm not going to let one disappointment discourage me."

A short time later she came to Mercy Hospital. A sweet-looking young woman sat at the visitors' desk.

"Do you wish to visit someone?" she asked, smiling.

"Yes, if he's a patient here," Nancy replied, and gave the name Clyde O'Mayley.

The young woman consulted her roster, then shook her head. "No one by that name is here now."

Nancy asked, "Would it be possible for you to find out if he stopped in your clinic during the past three or four days?"

The young woman nodded and dialed an extension. After a brief conversation, she told Nancy that the man she was trying to locate had not come to the Mercy clinic.

Nancy thanked her for being so helpful and left the hospital. Across the street she noticed a sign indicating a doctor's office.

"I'll start with him and then go on to other doctors in town asking them if Clyde O'Mayley has been to them for treatment."

The young detective approached the building, pressed the doorbell, and then walked in as a small sign over the bell directed. She was surprised to find no patients waiting. A nurse, who came from an inner room, announced that the doctor would not be in for another hour.

"I just stopped here," said Nancy, "to ask a question. I'm sure you can answer it."

She told about her search for Clyde O'Mayley, whom she suspected might have ornithosis. "I'm trying to locate him. Has he been here recently?"

"I think not," the nurse replied, "but I'll check and make sure."

She disappeared into the inner office and returned in a few moments. "No, he hasn't consulted the doctor."

Nancy asked if the woman had a list of all the doctors in town. "I should like to inquire at each office," she added.

The nurse said she was sorry but there was no printed list.

"Then may I look at the classified pages in

your phone book?" Nancy requested, certain that all the local physicians would be listed.

Nancy took a notebook and pencil from her handbag. When the nurse brought the book, Nancy copied the names and addresses. There were twelve.

"I hope you find the man you're looking for," the nurse said, after the young detective had thanked her. She smiled. "Is he a special friend?"

"No. Just the opposite. That's why I'm trying to find him. The police are looking for Clyde O'Mayley. If he should ever come in here, please call Harper headquarters."

The woman looked a bit startled that such a lovely and wholesome girl would be trying to track down a criminal, but she made no comment and said good-by.

For the next hour Nancy went from office to office. Some of the doctors worked in their own homes, others in office buildings. Finally Nancy, very weary, looked at her list.

"Only three more to go," she thought. "I guess Hannah will prove to be right. I'm not going to find that needle in this haystack."

Nancy drove to the next address. At the doctor's office she was surprised to be greeted by a young nurse who had been in grade school with her.

"Evelyn Hatch!" she exclaimed. "So you're a nurse."

"I'm in training. I work here afternoons."

"We lost track of each other after you moved to Harper," Nancy remarked.

"I can't believe it! Nancy Drew! I've missed seeing you. How is everything?"

"Oh, I keep busy," Nancy replied.

Evelyn grinned. "Are you still doing detective work?"

Nancy nodded. "That's why I'm here."

"The doctor's not in just now," Evelyn told her. "Is there something I can do to help you?"

Nancy told her about trying to find the man named Clyde O'Mayley who might have come for treatments for ornithosis. "Was he here?" she asked hopefully.

"Is he a criminal?" Evelyn asked.

"Well, yes, sort of," Nancy answered.

"Then I may have an interesting clue for you," Evelyn said. "There was a man in here who gave the name of Arthur Clyde. He did have ornithosis."

"What did he look like?" Nancy asked.

Evelyn's description fitted the wanted man. Nancy was thrilled. "Is he supposed to come back?"

The nurse told her that the patient had made an appointment for the following afternoon. "It's at four o'clock."

"I think I'll report this to Chief Pepper," Nancy remarked. "He can assign plainclothesmen to watch your office and nab the man if he's Slick Fingers."

"Who?" Evelyn asked.

Nancy laughed. "Oh, that's Clyde O'Mayley's nickname in the underworld."

Evelyn wagged her head. "Nancy Drew, you're really something! When I knew you in school you gave me the impression you would become a professional dancer, not a detective."

The two chatted for a while, then Nancy said she would go on to Harper Police Headquarters and then home.

"By the way, did the man have any identifying marks on him so we could trace him more easily if he doesn't show up tomorrow?"

"Yes, he did have one," Evelyn answered. "I was quite intrigued. On the top of his left arm he had a small tattoo. It was unusual, not like any I had ever seen before."

"What was it?" Nancy asked her.

"A circle with a cross in it. The vertical and horizontal lines extended fully from one side of the circle to the other."

Nancy caught her breath. This was the symbol used by Merv Marvel! She said nothing to Evelyn, but wondered if he and Slick Fingers were pals. Then a second thought came to her. Perhaps Merv had mesmerized Slick Fingers and got him to consent to the strange mark being tattooed on him.

"It must have been done recently," Nancy decided, "because the description of him on record did not mention a tattoo." Aloud she said, "Evelyn, this is important information. Thanks a lot. Let's try to meet again soon."

"I'd love to," her old school friend replied as Nancy left.

She went directly to see Chief Pepper. He greeted her with a smile and said, "I'm glad you dropped in. The fingerprints on the can of chloroform were definitely those of Slick Fingers. And have you brought me a new lead on him?"

The young detective puckered her mouth into a half-grin and said, "Yes, I have."

The chief listened attentively to her story. At the end he commented, "Every time I hear about your latest discoveries, I admire your sleuthing ability a little more. This bit of your detective work is excellent. I'll station men to watch the doctor's office and hope we can nab Slick Fingers."

Nancy said, "If he doesn't show up, can't your men locate him by looking for a man with the strange tattoo?"

"It's an excellent clue," the chief said. "We'll certainly use it."

Nancy arose and said good-by. As she was walking toward her car, she saw Oscar Thurston's assistant, Rausch, coming toward her. She waited for him.

"Oh hello," he said. "Say, I'm certainly glad I met you."

After greeting him, Nancy waited for the man to proceed. He went on to say that Kammy had phoned the Thurstons just before he had left the house.

"She was terribly upset," Rausch said. "Her pet wryneck, Petra, has disappeared!"

"What! How?" Nancy asked.

"Someone must have sneaked into her room in the college dorm and opened the cage. The window was open but there's no clue as to whether the bird got loose and flew away or was stolen."

"That's a shame," said Nancy. "How long ago did this happen?"

Rausch said apparently it had occurred during the morning. Kammy made the discovery at lunchtime when she returned to her room after class.

"She is heartbroken," Rausch went on, "and more than that she's fearful. You know Kammy thinks of that wryneck as if it were a Eurasian pal of hers. Now she's convinced she'll be jinxed. In fact," Rausch went on, "she told Oscar that she has already had some bad luck."

"What kind?" Nancy queried.

Rausch said that Kammy would not divulge what it was. Then he gazed steadfastly at Nancy and declared, "Maybe you can find out."

CHAPTER XII

The Double Jinx

As soon as Nancy heard of Kammy's problem, she wanted to rush out to Harper University and find her.

"She seems to trust me," the young detective thought. "Maybe she'll tell me what the bad luck is that has come to her.

As Nancy walked to her car with every intention of going to Harper University she suddenly became extremely weary. She felt light-headed and realized that she had to force herself either to walk or to think fast.

"I'd better not drive very long feeling this way," she concluded. "What in the world is the matter with me?"

Deciding that she should go home and rest, Nancy turned her car toward the highway that led to River Heights. By the time she reached her own house, Nancy was better and told herself she was probably imagining the weariness.

"But I'm hot."

Hannah Gruen was just coming from the second floor. "How's Ned?" Nancy asked her.

The housekeeper replied that she was glad to report Ned was feeling much better. "I guess the fever is going away." She smiled. "Nancy, I'm sure it will be all right for you to spend a little time with Ned. Your father won't be home to dinner. Suppose I fix the meal on two trays and you and Ned can eat together."

"That will be great," Nancy said. "I have so much to tell him about the mystery."

Still feeling warm, she took a shower and changed her clothes. Then she went into Ned's room.

"Hi!" she said. "I'm certainly glad you're more like your old self. You know you gave all of us quite a scare."

Ned grinned, then said, "I'm sorry I frightened you, but I sure felt terrible for a while. It was kind of fun, though, being waited on and mothered by Hannah. That may never happen again!"

Nancy laughed. "Don't become ill just to try us out!"

She now turned serious and told what she had found out that day. Ned was astounded at the amount of sleuthing she had done, and said he was sorry he had not been able to help.

"But I'll make up for it," he promised. "Tell me more about Kammy."

Nancy told him all she knew. "I want to visit the university and talk to her. And also, if Petra, her wryneck, isn't found soon, I want to hunt for it."

Nancy did not add that the reason she had not gone to the university was because she had been extremely weary. The same feeling began to return and she told herself it must be because she was hungry.

Hannah appeared with two individual portable tables on which were piping hot chicken broth and delicious fruit salad arranged artistically on beds of lettuce leaves.

The food looked delicious, but suddenly Nancy had no appetite. She forced herself to eat something but was so sleepy she could not finish. Finally she confessed her tiredness to Ned.

"I guess I've just been running around too much," she said. "I'm sorry, but I can hardly keep my eyes open. If you'll excuse me, I'll rest for a little while."

Ned looked disappointed. "Hannah promised a surprise. I think it's some kind of croquette with a spicy cream sauce."

Nancy did not know what to say. Her eyes now were half closed and they burned. Again she murmured, "I'm sorry," and went to her room.

Hannah came to her doorway a few minutes later and asked Nancy if she was ill.

"Oh no," Nancy assured the housekeeper. "Just dreadfully sleepy."

"Then you take a nice nap," Hannah Gruen told her. She went out into the hall and closed the door.

The housekeeper expressed her concern to Ned. But when he told her Nancy's remark about overdoing, the woman conceded the girl's conclusion was probably true. Nevertheless, Hannah was concerned about Nancy's symptoms but tried to dismiss her anxious thoughts.

"She never lets up."

Nancy undressed and went to bed. She fell into a deep sleep but awakened about midnight, her face burning. She felt very sick. Finally she decided to go tell Hannah Gruen.

Nancy slowly made her way down the hall and opened the door to the housekeeper's room. To her surprise Hannah was not asleep. She was propped up in bed reading.

"Oh, Hannah," said Nancy, "would you mind coming to my room? I feel so ill."

The kindly woman jumped up, put on her robe and slippers, and followed Nancy back to her bedroom.

She turned on the bright light and peered at the girl. "Nancy, I believe you have picked up the same thing Ned has!" she exclaimed. "I'm sure you are having an attack of ornithosis. You might say that now there's a double jinx on this house!"

Mr. Drew had heard the talking and had come to Nancy's room. When he was told her symptoms, he agreed with Hannah.

"It's a good thing none of us is superstitious," he said. "If we were, it would be easy to believe that a devil is working against some of us."

"I'm not so sure one isn't," Nancy spoke up feebly. "But who is he?"

Seconds later she fell asleep. Her father and Hannah conferred as to whether they should give her some of Ned's medicine or telephone the doctor. Mr. Drew decided they ought to call the physician first.

When Dr. Black heard of Nancy's condition, he said, "I'll drop over early in the morning. If Nancy is asleep now, don't awaken her, but later give her one dose of Ned's medicine."

At seven o'clock the next morning he came to the house and said indeed Nancy did have ornithosis. "Fortunately her case is lighter than Ned's, so she'll be up and around just about when he is."

After the doctor had gone, Mr. Drew talked with Hannah in the kitchen. "If whoever is behind this so-called jinxing hears about Nancy and Ned being ill, he'll be laughing at us. I was engaged by Oscar Thurston to straighten out the problems of the land deal, and now my own daughter has come down with a disease that I'm sure a troublemaker gave to the birds in their food and water."

Hannah said, "Don't forget that Clyde O'Mayley has ornithosis too." The lawyer nodded.

By noontime Nancy felt well enough to talk on her bedside telephone. She called Bess and George to tell them what had happened.

"I certainly hope you girls don't catch this virus," she said. "And, by the way, the fingerprints on the chloroform can were Slick Fingers'."

"Hypers!" exclaimed George. "Now we're getting some place. Bess and I feel fine. We're all ready to work. What can we do?"

Nancy replied, "The next councilman I was going to interview is Thomas Winnery. Suppose you do it. You know what to say to him."

The two girls promised to set off at once on their assignment. Mr. Winnery was the owner of the *Harper Times*, an excellent newspaper with a wide circulation.

Bess and George found the tall, ginger-haired man seated behind a large, cluttered desk in a wood-paneled office. He was very pleasant and easy to talk to. After introducing themselves, George said they had come to him at the request of Nancy Drew.

"The three of us," she went on, "are very interested in Mr. Thurston's zoo and aviary. We hear that there's a possibility it may all be destroyed and apartment houses built on the site."

"That's right," Mr. Winnery replied. "New industry is moving into the area and soon we'll need a lot of extra housing."

Bess spoke up. "Don't you think the development would be more attractive if the high-rise buildings faced on a man-made lake and if there were also a swimming pool, a park, and a playground?"

Mr. Winnery said he had not thought about this idea but he supposed it had merit. "Is this what you're proposing that the High Rise company do?"

Bess nodded. "We would like to see even more than that. If Mr. Thurston's buildings were on the other side of the lake and all the birds and animals were left there, don't you think it would be a marvelous attraction for children and guests?"

Mr. Winnery sat back in his swivel chair, folded his fingers in front of his face and then put his hands down again. "I admit I can envision great possibilities," he replied. "Who's idea is this?"

Together Bess and George answered, "Nancy Drew's."

Mr. Winnery remarked that the young lady must be very artistic. "Tell her to draw a sketch of her plan for me. If she can include as many apartment buildings as the present plans call for, I will speak to the other councilmen about the suggestion."

George was exuberant. "And maybe—maybe you could run some editorials in your paper approving the change?"

The newspaper owner laughed. "Not so fast, young lady. This is a lot for me to digest. But you can tell Nancy Drew for me that I will give the idea favorable consideration." Bess and George came away from Mr. Winnery's office delighted.

While they had been talking to him, George had noticed that the door had twice been silently opened a couple of inches and a pair of eyes had peered in.

"Was an office boy or clerk waiting to find out when his boss would be free?" George asked herself. "Or was he listening to all the conversation with an ulterior motive in mind?"

By the time the girls reached the hall, the listener was far down the corridor. He quickly turned the corner out of sight.

"He certainly acts as if he's trying to avoid us," Bess commented.

As she and George neared the front office, a young man stepped from behind the reception counter. He smiled and said, "I'm Gus. Mr. Winnery phoned and asked me to show you around if you were interested."

George said at once, "I am." Bess had no particular desire to see the plant, but offered to go along.

Gus opened a door and led them into a big room

with several small, hand-operated printing presses on one side. In the middle of the room were great open shelves stacked with pastel-colored paper and cardboard.

"This is the room where jobbing is done," the guide explained. "We make posters, flyers, and signs. These are platen presses. They are named for the flat metal plates on them which press the paper against the inked type."

Bess remarked, "I see lots of big cans of ink, and some are open."

"This ink," Gus said, "is more like paste than liquid and there are various colors. Over on those shelves are large pots of glue. And now I'll show you our big roll presses."

The two girls followed the young man out a side door that led to the parking lot. They walked across it and entered another long, low building.

"What an enormous press!" George exclaimed when they were inside. "Is this where you print the local paper?"

"Yes. The press operates by electricity. This particular one," Gus continued, as the girls looked at the long green machine, "can run six huge rolls of paper."

He pointed to a corner of the room where bolts of white paper, six feet long, were piled up, ready for use.

"That giant tank to one side is called Big

Bertha," Gus said. "It holds the black ink used in the printing."

The girls gazed at the enormous upside-down cylinder with a funnel-like bottom. Bess declared she had never seen so much ink in her life.

"Sometime," said George, "I'd like to come back while the presses are working."

"It is quite a sight," Gus told her. "But there's a great deal of noise too. You wouldn't like that."

Just then a bell rang twice. Gus said this was a call for him and he would have to leave. "Look around some more if you like. You know the way out."

After he had gone, Bess remarked, "I've seen enough. Let's go!"

At that moment something flew through the air and landed on top of her head. Quickly she put up her hand.

"Ugh!" she cried out. "It's some of that horrible glue!"

George went to help her cousin. Before she could reach her, a second glob of goo shot at lightning speed toward her. It landed with a squishy sound on the side of her face. It was red ink!

CHAPTER XIII

A Near Capture

FOR a few moments Bess and George were stunned. As they eyed the mess on each other's faces and clothes, they could only stare perplexed. Why should anyone have attacked them in this mean fashion?

Gus had heard them cry out and now ran back to the girls.

George burst out, "Who did this? Whoever it was, I'd like to tell him off!"

"I don't know," Gus said. "Come with me and we'll try to clean off this ink and glue."

"I think," said George, "that the person I saw outside Mr. Winnery's office was listening to our conversation. And I'll bet he's responsible for this, because he doesn't want High Rise's project stopped."

Bess agreed and asked Gus if he knew who the eavesdropper might have been.

"No, I don't," he replied. "What did he look like?"

George described him as a tall slender youth of about seventeen with a shock of blond hair. "He was wearing a red sweater and dark pants."

Gus said there was no employee at the newspaper office who fitted that description. "I suppose he slipped in here."

The young man stopped at a telephone and called a secretary named Claudia to come at once. When she saw the girls she gasped in amazement at their appearance, then asked them to follow her to the women's lounge.

Removing the ink and the glue from the sweaters was an impossible task. "Anyway," Claudia said, "you can at least wash your faces and hands."

This proved to be a hard job. The girls found it necessary to use cream, then pumice soap to remove the spots. When the three came outside, Mr. Winnery was waiting for them.

"I just heard what happened to you," he said to Bess and George. "It's a shame. I'll buy you girls new sweaters. Would you like to wait here while my secretary goes to a shop and gets them, or would you rather go home and pick them out later?"

Bess and George told Mr. Winnery this was not necessary. "You're not responsible, so why should you buy new sweaters?" He was so insistent, though, that they finally consented.

"I'd rather go home now and get mine later," George told him, then gave the newspaper owner a description of the suspicious youth.

Mr. Winnery frowned. "I think I know whom you're referring to. He doesn't work here, but came to the office on an errand."

"Who is he?" George asked.

Mr. Winnery hesitated before replying. Finally he said, "I don't want to get this person into trouble, but I'm sure the boy is Spike Hinchcliff. He's the son of one of the councilmen. He tries to be a detective but always fouls things up and makes people mad."

George asked, "Are you implying that his father made him come here to spy on Bess and me? But how would Mr. Hinchcliff have known about our plans?"

"I wouldn't go that far in my guessing," Mr. Winnery answered. "More likely Spike spotted you and decided to follow. I'm sure his father wouldn't approve."

Bess and George said good-by and went to their homes at once, but they planned to visit Nancy and report their adventure as soon as callers were allowed.

Fortunately her case of ornithosis was such a light one that two days later the cousins were able to tell her and Ned directly about their adventure at the newspaper office. Nancy was shocked at the brashness of the youth who had thrown the ink and the glue.

Ned was incensed. "That boy must be nuts!" he remarked. "It was such a senseless thing to do. And what did it accomplish?"

Nancy said that Spike's behavior might boomerang and help turn the tide for her father's side. "Spike is bound to tell his dad what he had overheard Bess and George talking about and how they were winning the newspaper owner to their side. Then when Mr. Hinchcliff finds out about the mean trick, he may feel sorry and accept our way of thinking about High Rise's project."

Ned and the other girls smiled and Ned remarked, "Nancy, you're always an optimist, aren't you? But I like your reasoning. How will we know what's happening between Spike and his father?"

Nancy grinned. "I'll give Dad that job."

She called him at once and within half an hour the young detective had an answer. Mr. Drew said he had been in touch with various councilmen and had interesting news for his daughter.

"That ink- and glue-throwing fellow definitely was Spike Hinchcliff. I understand his father is very embarrassed by the episode and has reprimanded his son. Here's even bigger news! Bess and George have won Mr. Winnery over to our side completely. When the council meets to vote on High Rise's project, he's going to propose your plan, Nancy. And he still wants a sketch of it."

"That's great!" she exclaimed. "I'll send one right away."

Bess and George were thrilled to learn that their trip to the newspaper office had brought positive results.

George grinned. "It was worth having ink thrown at me!"

"I'll never forget that goo in my hair!" Bess declared. "But, Nancy, I'm happy we were able to help you and your dad on the case."

After the cousins left, Ned asked Nancy if any word had come from the police about Slick Fingers.

"No. I guess he didn't show up at the doctor's office," Nancy replied.

Ned said he must return to college for a couple of days to attend to some fraternity business. "But I'll be back," he added. "Maybe I'll bring Burt and Dave with me."

Nancy said this would thrill Bess and George and together the six of them should be able to solve the mystery in a short time. Ned thanked Hannah Gruen profusely for all her nursing care and for taking a chance on becoming ill herself.

"Oh, I wasn't worried," the housekeeper remarked, smiling. "It was a pleasure to wait on you, Ned. You're a very good patient—no trouble at all."

He gave her a rewarding hug and a kiss. Then Nancy walked with him to his car.

"Take it easy, Nancy," Ned warned her. "When I return, I want you to be in tiptop condition."

"I promise," Nancy replied, smiling.

Ned opened the driver's door. Glancing at the car seat, he asked, "What's this?"

He picked up a small sheet of paper. On it, crudely drawn, was a small circle inscribed with a cross. He and Nancy stared at it, then Ned remarked, "Jinxed again!"

"It looks that way," Nancy agreed. "Of course we're not superstitious, so whoever is trying to jinx us is getting no place. Just the same, Ned, please be very careful while driving, and watch out for tricksters."

Nancy took the paper. After Ned had said goodby and pulled out of the driveway, she stared at the sheet. It was evident from the unevenness of the picture that the bad luck sign had been drawn hurriedly.

As Nancy entered the house, the phone began ringing. Bess was calling.

"On the way home George and I decided we'd like to take you on a picnic tomorrow. We'll go into a little woods where it's cool and quiet. Okay with you?"

"Sounds wonderful," Nancy answered. "I hope Dad and Hannah say it's all right for me to go."

To her delight both of them thought it would

do her good. "But don't let yourself get overtired," Hannah Gruen ordered.

The following morning Bess and George picked Nancy up. They had prepared the lunch and drove a few miles to a pretty wooded area with a creek running through it.

"We'll park here and walk a little way up the stream," Bess said as her cousin halted the car.

They had barely started the hike when Nancy stopped short and stared up at a branch of a large old maple tree.

"Look at that bird!" she exclaimed, and noted the snakelike way it twisted its head. "There's a wryneck straddling that branch. I wonder if it could be Petra."

The cousins followed Nancy's line of vision and agreed this might be Kammy's pet.

"We must capture the bird and take him with us!" Nancy said.

Before the other girls could stop her, she started shinning up the tree. Reaching the branch on which the wryneck sat, she began to coax him toward her with a low whistle and whispered words.

"Petra! Petra! Come here! Kammy misses you!"

The bird swung its head forward. He did not move but showed no sign of fright.

"He must be Petra!" Nancy thought. "Come, come!" she said.

Nancy began crawling along the limb toward

"Nancy!" Bess screamed.

the bird. She had almost reached him when the girls heard a cracking sound.

"Nancy!" Bess screamed.

"Jump! Quick!" George cried out as they watched the branch begin to split away under Nancy's weight.

As the wryneck flew off and there was another loud cracking sound, Nancy raised herself up to grab the limb above her. She was not a moment too soon. The one on which she had been crawling crashed to the ground.

Bess had covered her eyes with her hands, fearing the worst, but sighed in relief as she now saw Nancy pulling herself hand over hand toward the trunk of the old maple. In less than a minute she had shinned to the ground.

"Thank goodness," Bess exclaimed in relief. "Nancy, are you all right?"

"Yes, but I'm disappointed," she replied.

"Disappointed about what?" Bess queried.

Nancy said she was sorry to have lost her chance to capture the wryneck. She was sure he was Kammy's pet.

George suggested that Nancy relax a bit while they ate their lunch. "Maybe the bird will come back here and then Bess and I can try to capture him. You're still too weak to climb trees and chase birds."

The wryneck did not return, however, though the girls dawdled over the picnic for nearly an hour. Finally Bess said that perhaps Nancy had had enough excitement for one day and should return home.

"No, no," the young detective said quickly. "Won't you please drive to Harper University? I want to tell Kammy that we think we saw Petra. She can come here and try to catch him."

When the girls arrived at her dormitory, they went upstairs. Kammy's door was closed, so Nancy knocked.

"Come in," said a weak voice.

Nancy opened the door and the three callers entered. Kammy lay on a cot and her eyes were reddened and swollen from crying.

Nancy walked over and hugged the Eurasian girl. "I've brought you some good news," she said. "We believe we saw Petra in the woods. We'll give you directions to the spot."

"Oh, I hope you're right," said Kammy. "If he returns to me, I won't be responsible for breaking a long family tradition of keeping a wryneck."

Bess was a little surprised that Kammy did not seem happier that she might find Petra. Finally she burst out, "Kammy, we thought you'd be delighted to hear about Petra."

"Oh I am, I am," Kammy assured her. "But that is not my big worry now. Something awful has happened! I'm going to be arrested!"

CHAPTER XIV

Strange Hiding Places

"ARRESTED? For what?" Nancy asked Kammy, wondering if she had heard the girl right.

Sadly Kammy told Nancy, Bess, and George that a message had been sent to Professor Saunders accusing her of being a thief. "They say I stole and sold several specimens from the Harper University Museum!"

"Who sent the note?" Nancy inquired.

Kammy said it had not been signed. "But that doesn't make any difference. The birds are missing. Oh, girls," Kammy said, a little catch in her voice, "I didn't take them."

"Of course you didn't," George told her. "That was a wicked thing for someone to do."

Kammy burst into tears, "I have not harmed anyone and I cannot see why the person would deliberately tell a lie about me."

Nancy put an arm around her distressed friend.

"Kammy," she said, "here in America people are given a chance to prove their innocence before they're arrested. Please don't worry."

Nancy stood up. She suggested that Bess and George tell Kammy about everything that had happened recently, while she went to speak to Professor Saunders.

"All right," George agreed.

She engaged Kammy in conversation as Nancy quietly went out the door. She hurried to the professor's office and fortunately found him in. He was correcting summer students' term papers.

"Oh hello, Nancy Drew!" he greeted her. "I'm glad to see you. Anything new on the Thurston case?"

Nancy chuckled. "One big problem is now over. A friend of mine and I who were helping with the Thurston birds both caught ornithosis."

"How unfortunate!" the professor exclaimed. "Does Kammy know this?"

"I'm afraid not. She hasn't been in touch with the Thurstons, but two friends of mine who drove me here are telling her now."

Gradually Nancy turned to the subject uppermost in her mind and mentioned how upset Kammy was.

"She tells me she's going to be arrested for stealing and selling birds from the museum."

To Nancy's amazement the professor laughed heartily. Then he sobered.

"Poor Kammy! Did she take that note seriously?" he asked. "Since it was unsigned, I assumed it was meant as some kind of a hoax or joke. It's true that several valuable, rare birds disappeared from the museum. But it would not occur to me that Kammy had taken them."

"Then I have your permission to tell her not to worry any more?" Nancy asked. "And that she's not going to be arrested?"

"Please do. Tell her I'm exceedingly sorry this has happened. Kammy has seemed very sad lately but she never gave a reason for her moodiness and in fact she rarely talks."

The professor went on to say that he had found the Eurasian girl charming but very mysterious.

"Mysterious?" Nancy repeated. "How?"

Professor Saunders pointed to a pile of themes pushed to one side of his desk. "My students had an assignment and of all those I have read so far, Kammy's is superior to the rest."

Nancy wondered what this remark had to do with his thinking Kammy was mysterious. In a moment he explained.

"Near the end of her paper, I found a sheet which had been inserted. The paper did not match the others and there was no handwriting on it, just a drawing."

Professor Saunders stood up and started looking through the pile of papers. Presently he came to Kammy's and pulled it out. After flipping over several pages, he showed one of them to Nancy. On the inserted sheet was a large circle in which a cross had been drawn!

Professor Saunders looked at Nancy. "Have you any idea what this means and why Kammy would have put such an unrelated piece in this theme?"

Nancy told him that it was said to be a bad luck symbol but admitted that she was baffled too. "I doubt that Kammy inserted it herself," she said.

Professor Saunders looked at Nancy, puzzled. "My office is locked and no one but me has access to these papers."

The young detective thought a moment, then said, "The person who stole the birds from your museum perhaps could have access to your office also."

"That's possible," he agreed. "It might be a lead for the police. Apparently the thief is an enemy of Kammy's."

Nancy told the professor that the same symbol had been left in various places, including the Thurston home, the ballet director's desk, and Ned Nickerson's car. The professor was astounded.

"This whole case is more serious and mysterious than I realized," he remarked.

Nancy did not want to reveal any more of the results of her father's investigation, so she stood up and said she must hurry back to Kammy and tell her the good news.

"By all means," he replied.

When Nancy reached the dormitory, she found Kammy, Bess, and George talking animatedly. They stopped at once and looked up at Nancy.

"Good news!" the young detective exclaimed and rushed over to hug Kammy.

After she had delivered Professor Saunders' message, the Eurasian girl smiled. "Oh, I am so happy about this," she said. "Now I must find Petra! Please, could you take me to the place where you saw him?"

"We'd be glad to, but first I want to tell you something," Nancy replied. "Mr. and Mrs. Thurston need you very much at the farm, Kammy. The danger of the disease spreading among the rest of the birds is over. It will be perfectly safe for you to go back, and for you to take Petra if you find him."

"But I am afraid I bring bad luck to the Thurstons," she said.

Nancy insisted that this could not be true and that Oscar Thurston at least would not accept such an excuse.

"You know his wife is superstitious and believes in weird signs and omens and probably can be mesmerized. If she refuses to cooperate about selling the farm, someone may threaten to put a curse on her. We mustn't allow this to happen."

Kammy thought over the girl's comments a few seconds, then said, "Nancy, you are an amazing person. I feel so much better now. When we get to the front hall, will you telephone to the Thurstons and ask if they really want me to come back?"

Nancy was delighted. "And if they do, will you go?"

"Yes."

When Nancy phoned the Thurston home, Oscar answered. He said it would be wonderful if Kammy would return. Both he and his wife missed her very much and her help was invaluable. Nancy passed the complimentary message along to Kammy, whose face lighted up.

"I am so happy!" she said, and picked up Petra's large cage. "Now we find my lovely bird!"

As the girls left the building, she tucked her arm into Nancy's and said, "I just feel that some terrible spell has left me. I must not let it take possession of me again."

Nancy, Bess, and George exchanged satisfied glances. This truly was good news!

On the way to George's car, Kammy stopped at the housing office to arrange permission to return to the Thurston farm. Then the girls rode to the spot where they had seen the wryneck.

"Look!" Bess exclaimed. "Petra is sitting on that broken limb!"

When Kammy alighted from the car, she slowly walked toward her pet. He did not fly away nor even move. When she opened the bird-cage door, he flew to it and hopped inside. The Eurasian girl began speaking to him in her native language. The bird jumped around the cage excitedly, apparently understanding her words.

The next moment she reached in and took Petra in her hands. Lovingly she stroked his feathers.

Suddenly Petra began to show signs of being uncomfortable, so Kammy held him by his feet. The bird stretched his wings wide. His owner gave a little gasp.

Taped underneath one wing was a tiny package!

George spoke up. "So Petra was stolen!" she remarked angrily.

Carefully Kammy detached the little package, returned the pet to his cage, and closed the door. As the girls watched, she unwrapped the package, looked at the object inside, then burst into tears.

CHAPTER XV

Fingerprint Proof

"KAMMY, what's the matter?" Nancy asked as her Eurasian friend continued to sob.

Bess and George were trying to see what she was holding, but the girl had doubled her fist, hiding the object from view.

A few seconds later Kammy stopped crying and opened her hand. On the palm lay a gorgeous ring. She slipped it onto her thumb and they all stared at the golden band. Mounted on the top were three circles of gems. The outer one was sparkling green emeralds. The middle one contained glistening yellow topaz and the inner circle was set with small diamonds clustered around a larger one.

"It's fabulous!" Bess exclaimed. "But why would it be taped under Petra's wing?"

"I do not know," Kammy replied. "This is a family heirloom which I brought with me when

I came to this country. It disappeared about a month ago and I thought I had lost it. I am very puzzled now—and a little frightened too."

"Why should getting the ring back frighten you?" Bess asked her.

Kammy said it was not the ring itself which bothered her, but the strange way in which it was returned. Had someone found it? Had an enemy stolen it? But if so, why would he or she want to give the valuable piece back?

Bess gave a great sigh. "Oh, if Petra could only talk, he could solve the whole thing!"

Nancy, seeing that Kammy was becoming more upset, decided to change the subject. "Since you're going back to the Thurstons, and if George doesn't mind, why don't we drive over there now and leave Petra?"

Kammy agreed and George said she would be happy to take them all.

But Bess was concerned about how Nancy was feeling. "Maybe you've had enough excitement for one day. You were supposed to take it easy, and I wouldn't say you have."

Nancy laughed and assured the others she felt all right. "I'm sure I've recovered completely."

The Thurstons were delighted to see the girls. They especially welcomed Kammy cordially and said they were delighted she was coming back.

"My birds haven't seemed entirely happy since

you left," Oscar told her. "They don't sing or chatter much."

Kammy blushed. "It's good to hear that they missed me," she replied. "Is there some work I can do right now?"

"Not out in the cages," the man answered. "But—"

Mrs. Thurston interrupted him and said to the girls, "Oscar and I are very much alarmed!" She turned to her husband. "Show the girls that awful letter you got."

Oscar took it from the desk and read the contents aloud. The letter was from Mr. Ramsey Wright, president of the High Rise Construction Company. It was an order for the Thurstons to vacate the premises totally within a month.

"We are raising our price to you by one thousand dollars," the letter stated. "That should cover any loss you may have to take with the closing of your zoo and aviary."

Oscar put down the letter. "I don't want the money. I just don't want to leave here. Nancy, what can we do?"

The young detective offered to phone her father at once for his advice. Mr. Drew told her that Ramsey Wright had no business to send such a letter.

"Mr. Wright is just trying to take advantage of someone who does not know his rights under the law," he said. "Nancy, tell Oscar that no sale can be forced until after the town council has voted to grant the High Rise Construction Company authority to acquire the land."

Smiling, Nancy rejoined the group. She passed along her father's message and Mr. and Mrs. Thurston relaxed.

"Dad also told me something else," Nancy went on. "He received a phone call from Mr. Winnery, who said that he had convinced Mr. Hinchcliff, Mr. Ryan, and another councilman, Mr. Clifford, to vote for my alternate plan for the housing development."

Bess suddenly clapped her hands and said, "Hip, hip, hurrah!"

As the others grinned at her in amusement, she went on, "Now that makes four out of the five councilmen who are for Nancy's plan. Isn't that a majority?"

Oscar nodded. "Yes, it is, but in this case the council agreed some time ago that the vote would have to be unanimous."

"Humph!" said George. "That means we have one more man to convince."

Kammy said she must leave. "I'll take the bus back to the university and pick up my clothes that are there. I'll return as soon as I can."

George offered to take her but the Eurasian girl shook her head. "Nancy should go right home and crawl into bed. She looks very tired."

Nancy admitted that she was, so all the girls left. They had barely started off when Nancy said, "I'd like to stop at police headquarters and see if there's any news on the case."

Bess tried to convince her friend that she should not stop just now, but Nancy said the call would not take long.

Chief Pepper greeted her warmly and said, "No new leads on the Thurston case. But my men will keep on the alert for Slick Fingers."

Nancy thanked the chief for the information and left. Then George drove her directly to the Drew home.

When Nancy walked in, Hannah looked at her reproachfully. "Nancy, I think you've been doing something strenuous. You look exhausted and I suggest you get to bed at once."

"But, Hannah dear, I have so much news for you and Dad. Please let me eat some supper with you while I tell you what happened today, then I'll go upstairs."

Her audience of two alternately chuckled and looked alarmed as Nancy told the story of her near accident on a broken tree limb, the rescue of Petra and of Kammy's heirloom ring which had been returned so mysteriously.

Her father commented, "You had enough adventures in one day, Nancy, to last most people a week."

Nancy laughed. "Don't such things happen to

all detectives?" she asked, then kissed Hannah and her father good night. "Tomorrow I plan to call on Mr. Tabler, one of the councilmen, and find out which way he plans to vote on High Rise's proposed projects."

"I believe he owns a nursery," her father stated, "and High Rise wants to buy it. I hope you're planning to take Bess and George along for support."

The following morning Nancy called the cousins, who agreed to accompany her. Nancy offered to drive and pick them up. By the middle of the morning the three girls were nearing the town of Harper. They watched for signs to the Tabler Nursery.

"That's probably it off to the right where all those trees and bushes are growing in rows," Bess spoke up.

When they came to a narrow side road the girls saw the sign for which they were looking. They pulled into the rear yard of a farmhouse.

A large group of young boys and girls were running about, screaming and laughing. Nancy and her friends could not figure out what kind of game they were playing.

"What a noise!" Bess commented, holding her hands over her ears.

The three callers got out of the car. One boy about twelve who had been throwing a football into the air sent it whizzing directly at George.

Before it could hit her, she caught the ball neatly and tossed it back to him. He looked surprised.

"Good catch!" he said.

In the meantime Bess had dodged a toy airplane. One little girl, who had made a row of mud pies in a corner of the yard, now picked one up. She threw it straight at Nancy, who quickly jumped out of the way. The mud pie landed on another child. The rest of them giggled and several clapped.

A woman came from a rear door of the house. She told the children to quiet down.

Nancy asked for Mr. Tabler and learned that he was not at home. The young detective explained her reason for coming and said, "Will you please pass this information along to Mr. Tabler."

"I'll tell him, but it won't do any good. He's made up his mind about the Thurston property. It should be sold. The High Rise people are going to build another complex here. They have offered us a good price for this place.

"You see, these are not my children, but my grandchildren. They're here because there's no other place for them to go. The housing shortage is fierce. My own five children have already signed up for apartments at the Thurston place. They'll be built first. After that my husband and I could retire on the profit we'd get for this place, and move to a smaller house." She smiled. "Then maybe we'd have some peace and comfort."

Nancy had a hunch she could never convince Mrs. Tabler that her husband should vote against the High Rise Construction Company's plans. The young detective now used a completely different approach.

Turning toward the children, she said, "Have you ever been to Mr. Thurston's zoo and aviary?"

"No!" they shouted.

"Would you like to visit it with me right now?" Nancy asked. "That is, if your grandmother will let you go."

There were squeals of delight from the younger children and shouts from the older ones.

"Yes, yes!" they all replied.

Nancy turned to Mrs. Tabler. "Would it be all right with you?"

The woman thought a moment. "How would you get them all over there?"

"We can fit them into my car," Nancy replied. "The younger ones can sit on the laps of the older children."

"All right," Mrs. Tabler said.

Nancy opened the car door and at once the youngsters began to pile in. There were a few arguments but Nancy, Bess, and George soon settled them and in a short time Nancy was ready to leave.

The children waved to Mrs. Tabler and she called, "Have a good time!"

Nancy headed in the direction of the Thurston

farm. A motorcycle policeman passed her and all the children shouted and waved to him.

Five minutes later Nancy heard a siren. The sound grew louder. Looking in the rear-view mirror, she saw another policeman on a motorcycle coming at high speed toward her. Presently he pulled alongside and signaled her to stop. She did and looked at him questioningly.

"Young lady," he said, "don't you know the law?"

CHAPTER XVI

Nancy's Strategy

THE children in the car sat in silence, stunned by the sudden appearance of the policeman. Bess and George gasped at the idea he evidently was accusing Nancy of breaking the law!

"I think I know the traffic laws," she replied. "Is something the matter? Surely I wasn't speeding."

"No, you weren't. But you are still breaking the law. Your car is overcrowded." He looked inside. "My word, how many children are in here?"

Bess answered. "There are nine."

"And three adults," the policeman said. "By my arithmetic that adds up to twelve persons. The most your car can hold is six."

Nancy felt very uncomfortable.

Looking at the officer, she smiled and said, "I wasn't going far. These children are from the

Tabler place. I'm taking them only to the Thurstons' to see the birds and animals. Please let me go the rest of the way. I'll make sure two cars take the children back."

Silence followed. Finally one of the boys said, "Oh please, Mr. Policeman, we want to see the animals and everything."

A little girl piped up, "And she's a very nice lady to bring us."

The officer smiled. "Okay, it's obvious you're doing a good deed and you're not far from the Thurston place. But from now on, remember, no more than six people in this car."

Nancy thanked him and drove on. The children cheered and clapped. A little girl in the back seat leaned forward and put her hands on Nancy's shoulders. "I was afraid he was going to put you in jail. We wouldn't want that to happen!"

Nancy, Bess, and George were touched by the children's solicitude. Despite their pranks and annoyance to their grandmother, they were lovable. And with more training they could learn to act courteously to strangers.

Nancy was startled a moment later when one of the older girls asked Nancy, "Did that policeman try to jinx you?"

In amazement Nancy asked her, "What do you know about jinxes?"

"Oh," said the child, whose name was Sue, "a

man comes to Gram's house sometimes. He told us children if we didn't do as he says he'd put a jinx on us."

Nancy frowned. "You know he can't do that. It's a lot of nonsense."

"Is it?" Sue asked. "The man said he could have us turned into animals."

"That's right," a boy spoke up. "The jinx man said he could bring us all kinds of bad luck."

Nancy and her friends made no comment. They were convinced that the man had said this to frighten the children. But why?

Finally Nancy had an idea and asked, "What did this person want you to do?"

Sue replied promptly, "He wants us to tell Gram and Gramp that their house and the whole place has spooks and they should sell it."

"Spooks?" George repeated. "There are no such things."

"Oh, yes, there are," Sue insisted. "Janie and I saw one from our bedroom window."

The little girl named Janie added, "The spook was all white and leaped around the garden. Boy, could he jump high! Once he flew right across the big flower bed!"

The same thought rushed into the minds of Nancy, Bess, and George. The spook might be the specter who had swooped across the Thurstons' living room!

Nancy asked the children, "What was his name?

I don't mean the spook, but the other man who told you about these things."

"He was Mr. Mervman," Sue answered.

"Do you mean Merv Marvel?" Nancy suggested.

The children shook their heads and Janie said, "No, Mervman." Nancy and her friends were sure he was the ballet dancer who had been dismissed from the Van Camp troupe.

A few minutes later the car pulled into the Thurston farm. As the visitors piled out, Oscar came toward the group.

Nancy explained why she had brought the children and introduced them. "I told them of my idea for the housing development with your farm being kept as an aviary and zoo."

Oscar winked at her and then said, "Come with me, children. I'll show you the birds first."

Nancy herself was intrigued by the talk which followed. As they walked past the cages of rare parrots, with green, blue and red feathers, Oscar said, "Birds have an interesting bone structure. Their bodies are lightweight for flying because the bones are hollow and those in the wings have air sacs. Have you ever watched a bird take a running start and then lift into the air just like an airplane?"

The children shook their heads no. One boy named Jimmy asked, "What's that funny-looking bird?" He pointed.

"That's an Atlantic puffin," the bird owner

told him. He said that the bird, which had a very puffy chest and a hooked blue-and-red bill, was not exactly cuddly.

"Oh, I see a beautiful bird!" Janie cried out, pointing to a sleek one with a yellow stomach. The rest of its body was mostly covered with lustrous green feathers.

"That's an emerald cuckoo from Africa," Oscar told her. "Let's see if we can make him sing."

Oscar made a sound like *cuckoo, cuckoo.* The bird lifted its head, looked all around and then, to the children's delight, answered, "Cuckoo, cuckoo."

Jimmy was so intrigued he had put his face close to the cage. He remarked, "This is a fun place. I wish I could go in there."

Oscar said this would not be wise. "Strangers frighten the birds."

Presently they came to a cage of various breeds of hummingbirds. Many of the dainty little creatures were fluttering in midair, sipping something from the flowers of an artificial tree. Oscar explained that he filled the cups of the flowers each day with nectar.

"These tiny birds are amazing," he said. "They need a terrific amount of energy to make their wings work that fast.

"In proportion to its size a bird consumes a great deal more food than a man. For instance, a pigeon eats one-twentieth of its own weight daily. To equal this appetite a man would have to consume nine pounds a day, three times his average intake."

Bess remarked, "Then the old saying that a person eats like a bird isn't true."

"That's correct," said Oscar.

When the tour of the aviary was finished, Rausch met the visitors and led them to another part of the farm. There, behind a row of tall poplar trees, was the small zoo he managed.

The children laughed gleefully over the bears, whom they were allowed to feed. Next they went to see the deer, a pair of sleepy lions, and a giraffe whose neck was so long his head stuck out over the top of his pen.

"Couldn't he get away?" Janie asked.

Rausch said, "Not a chance. He'd have to get a running start to leap out and the pen is too small for that."

After the visitors had seen all the animals, Oscar invited his guests to the house for ice cream and cookies. Bess and George offered to help him serve, while Nancy talked with the children.

She began by asking, "Would you like to see this place destroyed?"

"No!" they all shouted loudly.

She told them that the man who called himself Mr. Mervman wanted to do this.

"How awful!" Janie exclaimed.

Nancy said she agreed and was working hard

to keep the town council from voting in favor of such a thing. "The builders want to put the apartment houses right here and destroy the Thurston farm.

"Will you do me a favor?" she went on. When they all said yes, she added, "Tell your Gram and Gramps how much you love this place and you want it to stay. Maybe you could write a letter to the newspaper and all of you sign it."

"We'll do it!" Janie cried out.

Just then Oscar Thurston came out of the kitchen with a tray of ice cream on sticks. Bess followed with a heaping plate of cookies.

After a while Nancy noticed that one ice-cream pop was still on the tray. "Who doesn't like ice cream?" she asked the children.

No one answered. She began to count and presently said, "Jimmy is missing."

At that moment they all heard a scream from the section where the birds were kept. Nancy ran outside and moments later was horrified to find that Jimmy had entered a cage.

A huge black raven, frightened and angry at the intrusion, was attacking him. Jimmy continued to scream as the bird's huge, cruel claws kept striking at him.

Nancy did not wait. Grabbing up an empty feed sack from the ground, the young detective opened the door of the cage and rushed inside!

CHAPTER XVII

Frightening Plunge

THE raven attacking Jimmy had a twenty-four-inch wingspread. Its huge unwebbed toes were digging into the little boy's back. The youngster was screaming and trying to reach the gate and safety.

As Nancy sped toward him, she unfolded the feed sack. The next moment she threw it over the bird's head and yanked the creature away from his victim.

"Run!" she yelled at Jimmy.

The boy needed no urging. He made a beeline for the doorway, still crying and screaming. He was met by Oscar, who had come on the run to find out what had happened. Bess was right behind and took charge of Jimmy.

The bird owner called, "I'll take care of the raven. Nancy, you hurry out of here!"

She paused a second to see how Oscar was going to manage the bird, which was trying with its beak and one leg to get the feed sack off its head.

Oscar spoke soothingly to the raven as he folded down its flapping wings and held the bird under one arm. He now removed the offensive sack and at once the bird stopped struggling.

"You're all right, Blackie," he said to the raven. "You're not hurt, and you were bad to attack the little boy. Now behave yourself," he added and let the bird go.

The raven immediately flew into a tree branch and gave a loud croaking call.

Nancy, eager to see how Jimmy was, hurried up to the house. Bess and George had already removed his shirt and were applying a soothing antiseptic lotion to the bleeding scratches. The child was still sobbing but Nancy was sure this was more from fright than injury.

Oscar came into the kitchen holding the tattered feed sack. "You were quick-witted to use this, Nancy." He smiled. "I'd better keep the bag handy in case another one of my birds gets out of hand!"

Jimmy was so interested in the conversation that he stopped crying. The boy said he would never go into a cage again. "This one wasn't locked like the others."

He now asked to be taken home. Bess promised they would do so as soon as she put a bandage and adhesive over the scratches.

Nancy mentioned to Oscar about being stopped

by a motorcycle policeman and agreeing to take the children home in two separate trips. At once the man offered to drive most of them in his large station wagon.

Nancy told them all to climb into the cars. "I'll join you in a minute." It had occurred to her that she should speak to Mrs. Thurston before leaving.

She went through the kitchen to the living room, expecting to find the woman in her wheelchair. It was empty and she was not in sight.

"Mrs. Thurston must be upstairs," Nancy concluded.

When she came outside Nancy mentioned this to Oscar. He smiled sadly. "I'm afraid Martha is worse. She doesn't want to come downstairs at all today."

"I'm dreadfully sorry," said Nancy. "Is she physically ill or just worrying too much?"

Oscar said that his wife was so upset over their future that she could not sleep and had no appetite.

"And now," he went on, "she can't face meeting anyone; otherwise, I would urge you to try consoling her. Well, let's go!"

He and Nancy got into their cars and rode off with the others. When they reached the Tabler place, the children jumped to the ground and ran up to their grandmother. She was seated in the yard.

Mr. Tabler appeared from the house. The tall,

slender nurseryman was introduced to Nancy, Bess, and George by his wife. Then Nancy introduced Oscar to the Tablers.

There was no chance for further conversation among the adults. The children began telling about Oscar's farm where there were animals and all kinds of birds.

"It was so exciting," said Janie, her eyes glowing happily. "Oh, please don't destroy that farm, Gramps."

Mr. and Mrs. Tabler looked at their grandchild in astonishment, then asked what she meant.

All the children took turns, trying to tell them and finally it was evident from their growing smiles that Gram and Gramps were impressed.

"I will come over to see you, Mr. Thurston," the nurseryman promised. "I understand the High Rise company wants to buy your entire property and put apartment buildings on it."

"Don't let them!" one of the boys shouted.

At that moment Mrs. Tabler realized that Jimmy had no shirt on and there were strips of adhesive on his back. "What happened to you?" she asked in concern.

Jimmy hung his head. "I didn't pay attention to the sign," he confessed. "It said to keep away from the cage but I wanted to see the big black bird, so I went in. He scratched me, but Nancy saved me."

Oscar said he was terribly sorry the accident had happened. "Jimmy was a brave boy and knew enough to put his arms over his eyes to protect them."

The little boy had been frightened because he expected to be punished. Now he smiled his thanks at Oscar. The Tablers did not reprimand their grandson and the others assumed that Gram and Gramps thought Jimmy had been punished enough.

As the three girls were leaving in Nancy's car, Mr. Tabler called, "I'll take your suggestion seriously, Miss Drew, about High Rise's development plans. Mind, I don't promise anything, though."

"I'm betting he'll vote to keep Oscar's place," Bess whispered.

George was inclined to agree but Nancy did not comment. She hoped intensely that the children would win him over.

When Nancy arrived home she was delighted to see Ned's car in the driveway. He said that his work at the college had not taken long, so he was able to return sooner than he had expected.

Grinning, he asked, "I hope you don't mind."

As Nancy made a face at him, he added, "What's new on the mystery that I can help you with?"

Nancy told him that she wanted to meet Mr. Ramsey Wright, the head of the construction company, and judge for herself what kind of a man he was. "Would you like to drive over to his office this afternoon?"

Ned nodded and Nancy immediately went to the telephone to make an appointment. She learned that the president of the High Rise Construction Company was not available. When Nancy said she had something important to talk to him about, the secretary told her, "He's going to lunch now. After that he'll be looking over one of his projects out in Tomkinsville."

"Thank you," Nancy said.

She and Ned told Hannah where they were going. At once the housekeeper said, "Have you heard about Tomkinsville?"

When they both said no, she told them that many people thought of it as a disaster area.

"In what way?" Nancy queried.

"There's a river running along the edge of it— nice and clear with a very pretty dam that ends in a deep falls. Along one bank, there used to be a lovely park with various kinds of recreational facilities and also boating and an area for swimming. But now it's all gone and they're expecting a lot of high-rise apartment houses to be built there."

Nancy was sorry to hear this. "The man who is behind it is the same one who wants to destroy the Thurston farm," she told Hannah.

The housekeeper pursed her lips. "There ought to be a law against permitting such things!"

Nancy and Ned made no comment but both

agreed. They had lunch, then went out to Ned's car and drove to Tomkinsville. After a couple of inquiries on where the park had been, Ned went in that direction. Reaching the site, they saw a bulldozer and crane already at work.

Nancy tried to speak to the drivers but the noise of the machinery was so loud it drowned her voice. The men made no attempt to turn off the engines and speak to them. Seeing a workman on foot a distance away, they walked over to him.

"Would you tell us please where Mr. Wright is?" she asked the man.

Instead of replying the man stared at her and then asked, "What are your names?"

Ned told him. The man continued to study Nancy and finally remarked, "Nancy Drew, eh? I've heard of you. You're an amateur detective, aren't you?"

"I've solved some mysteries," she answered.

The workman asked, "What do you want to see Mr. Wright about?"

"I have a message for him," she replied, and thought it best to say nothing more.

"I'll see if I can find him," the workman said. "Why don't you two walk down by the river? There's a dam a little way along. It's very pretty. I think you would enjoy seeing it."

As he went off, Nancy and Ned turned toward the water. They came to the river and started to walk downstream.

"Isn't this pretty?" Nancy asked. "It must have been a lovely park."

"It's too bad they're destroying it," Ned remarked.

The couple stopped to gaze at the rushing water. Suddenly they heard footsteps directly behind them and turned just in time to see a giant man leering at them. The next instant he put one of his great pawlike hands on each of the young people and gave them a tremendous shove. Nancy and Ned lost their balance and tumbled toward the water!

Being excellent swimmers they were able to twist their bodies into perfect dives. When they surfaced, the two had already been swept a good distance downstream. Battling hard against the strong current, they tried to turn toward shore but found this impossible to do.

"The dam is not far ahead with the high falls!" Nancy thought.

Ned was trying frantically to reach Nancy's side and help her. He could not make it.

A few moments later the two went over the dam!

Nancy and Ned held their breath as they were swept down the falls and prayed that they would not hit rocks. Fortunately neither did. They felt as if their lungs would burst before they were able to take in deep breaths of fresh air.

A little farther on the water became less turbu-

Nancy and Ned went over the dam!

lent, and Nancy and Ned swam to shore. Exhausted, they dragged themselves up the embankment and sat down.

"Thank goodness you're all right," Ned told her.

"I'm glad we're both okay," Nancy replied. "I was terrified that we might hit rocks."

She and Ned realized they had been very lucky. The weather was warm so they did not feel chilled. Both had lost their sandals and looked bedraggled. Nancy tried wringing the water from her hair and clothes.

Finally she smiled. "New-style bathing outfit. How do you like it, Ned?"

He laughed and said, "I'd hate to wear these clothes in a swimming meet! Nancy, do you realize that this time we were jinxed together? Do you suppose that means something?" A mischievous twinkle came into his eyes.

"Sure it means something," she echoed. "Another double jinx! Ned, I'm positive now that Mr. Ramsey Wright is the president in charge of hijinks. He doesn't do the work himself but employs people like this giant, and Slick Fingers and Merv Marvel."

She and Ned noticed a police car approaching. It stopped near them and a young state trooper stepped out.

"You're the two who went over the dam?" he asked.

"Yes."

"You must be mighty fine swimmers," he said. "Few people falling into the river near the dam would make it out alive."

"How did you know about us?" Ned asked him.

"A boy ran up to me and said he'd seen you."

Nancy explained that she and Ned had driven to the development to see Mr. Wright. "While we were looking at the river, a tall, muscular man came up and pushed us in!"

"What!" the officer exclaimed. "By the way, where is your car?"

Ned told him and the officer offered to take the couple back in the police car. As they neared the construction site, Nancy suddenly cried out:

"There goes that giant man now!"

CHAPTER XVIII

An Arrest

THE state trooper revved up his car and raced along the roadway toward the fleeing giant. The huge man turned his head. Realizing he was being pursued, the suspect turned away from the road and darted into the development.

"We mustn't let him get away!" Nancy cried out.

As the trooper stopped the car, she jumped out. Together she, the police officer, and Ned tore after the big man. Their speed far exceeded his and after a short race they caught up to him. The trooper clamped a hand on his shoulder.

"What's this all about?" the giant asked indignantly.

"Who are you?" the officer queried.

"My name's Nat Banner and I used to be a strong man in the circus. Now are you satisfied?"

The officer turned to Nancy and Ned. "Is this the fellow who pushed you into the water?"

"Yes," they answered together.

The trooper addressed the man again. "These young people might have drowned," he declared. "Did you attack them?"

Banner looked sullen. "I never saw these folks before in my life. Besides, I don't know what you're talking about. I didn't push anybody into the water."

When Nancy and Ned continued to insist that their identification was correct, the suspect said, "I was nowhere near the water. I can prove it by Mr. Wright." He looked off in the distance. "Here he comes now."

When the owner of the High Rise Construction Company joined the group, he asked what the trouble was. The giant whined, "These folks are sayin' I pushed 'em into the river. I never did any such thing. I wasn't near the water. You know that, don't you, Mr. Wright?"

"Of course you weren't. You were with me until just a few minutes ago," Mr. Wright said. "Banner is one of my trusted employees."

The trooper looked from one to another, then said to Nancy and Ned, "If this man says he's not guilty and you have no witnesses, there's no proof. What do you want to do about it?"

Mr. Wright stared angrily at Nancy. "You'd better drop this crazy charge."

Nancy thought she detected a double meaning in his words—they were intended as a threat for her not to pursue the issue any longer.

Not easily frightened, she changed her whole approach to the situation. Looking at Mr. Wright, she asked, "Would you two men mind walking down to the part of the river where we were pushed in? Maybe you could help us find the person responsible."

The High Rise owner and his massive employee glanced at each other, then Mr. Wright said, "I haven't much time to spend with you. But I'll go along."

The trooper was a bit curious but had no chance to ask the young detective what she had in mind. The whole group trailed her to the riverbank. There Ned and the trooper smiled. In the soft mud were long, deep footprints definitely made by the type of boot the giant was wearing.

"When Mr. Banner was running," Nancy said, "I noticed the ridges in the sole of his boot and the heel mark. These are the same."

Mr. Wright said quickly, "Lots of men wear boots like his. This match doesn't prove anything."

Ned spoke up. "I think it does. These boots are extra large. The depth of the last two prints near the river indicates that the person standing here had to sink his full weight in order to push one or two heavy objects into the water."

The trooper agreed. He asked Nancy and Ned if they wanted to prefer charges against Banner.

"Yes, we do," Ned answered.

There were strenuous objections from both Mr. Wright and his employee, but their opponents were insistent and the offender was taken away in the State Police car. After Nancy and Ned had been to headquarters to file their complaint, the trooper drove Nancy and Ned to the latter's car.

Ned had been driving for a little while when he began to laugh and said, "I've always told myself if I'm looking for danger and excitement, just go on an errand with you!"

Nancy grinned. "Now own up, Ned, you wouldn't have liked this afternoon half as much if it hadn't been full of excitement."

"Okay," he replied, "but please give me one hour to rest before you get me involved in another hair-raising mystery."

"I promise," Nancy said, laughing. "I might even give you two hours."

The two bantered all the rest of the way home. When Hannah saw them, she was astonished at their appearance. "What did you two do? Go swimming with your clothes on?"

"We sure did," Ned replied, and told what had happened to them.

Once more Hannah was aghast "That was dreadfully dangerous," she commented, frowning. "Such an ugly-tempered man should be kept behind bars until he's so old he can't push people into rivers!"

Nancy and Ned smiled. They loved the intenseness of Hannah's loyalty. Ned, chuckling, told the housekeeper he was beginning to agree that somebody had put a double jinx on Nancy and himself.

"If I were superstitious," said Hannah, "I could well believe that. First you both came down with ornithosis, then somebody flings you into a river."

Ned sighed. "Three times is out. I wonder what the next jinx will be."

"Well, I certainly hope this is the end," Hannah stated firmly. "By the way, I was reading something interesting the other day. Did you know that certain primitive people regarded their names as an integral part of their souls? To protect themselves from witchcraft, they kept their real names secret. They believed that no one could jinx them while they were using a fictitious name."

Nancy and Ned said they had never heard about this, though many of the common superstitions were familiar to them.

"I like the one about a person's left shoulder being the bad side of him," Nancy remarked. "That's why someone, seeing a new moon for the first time over his left shoulder, throws salt over that shoulder to reverse any bad luck it might bring."

Ned said he preferred the one about a person

carrying a rabbit's left hind foot for good luck. "I see one dangling now and then in a person's car." Then he asked, his eyes twinkling, "Knocking on wood is supposed to bring luck. Does this idea come from woodpeckers pecking at tree bark, hoping to have luck finding a juicy insect?"

Nancy and Hannah laughed. Then the housekeeper changed the subject.

"A phone call came today for you and the message was that tomorrow morning you will have a surprise. Now don't ask any more. That's all I can tell you."

It was not until midmorning the next day that they found out what it was all about. The front doorbell rang and both of them hurried to answer it. Bess, George, and two athletic-looking blond young men, Burt Eddleton and Dave Evans, who dated the cousins frequently, stood before them.

"Surprise!" they exclaimed. Bess added, "We've brought reinforcements and we're ready for a sleuthing job."

Nancy cried out, "How wonderful to see you!"

Ned kissed the girls and slapped the boys on the back.

Mr. Drew was still at home and said he was delighted to hear about the reinforcements. The group sat down for a second breakfast snack and discussed the mystery.

"What I'd like you to do is visit the High Rise Construction Company office and see what you can learn," Mr. Drew said. "Also I'd like you to investigate the sites on which Mr. Wright plans to build. I have a list of them."

The lawyer thought it best if the boys went to the High Rise company alone. Nancy and the other girls could visit the development areas and find out all they could about how the property had been acquired.

When the group was about to leave the house, the telephone rang. Nancy answered and the others heard her say, "I have nothing to tell you, and if you have finished, I'll say good-by." She hung up.

"Who was that?" her father asked.

Nancy explained that it was Mr. Wright, who had told her he had to pay a high sum to bail out his employee. "Then he said, 'If you and your friend don't retract your charge against Nat Banner, you'll be sorry!' " Nancy added with determination, "Well, I won't pay any attention to him," she concluded.

"He can't scare me either," said Ned. "Incidentally, while I'm at the High Rise office, I'd better not let him see me."

The others, however, expressed alarm. Mr. Drew begged his daughter and her friends to take extra precautions. They promised, then left the house. The boys went off in Burt's car, which would not be recognized by anyone connected with the High Rise personnel.

Nancy, Bess, and George headed for the first site on Mr. Drew's list. They could find nothing wrong or underhanded about the purchase, and the sellers had been willing to part with their property.

Another place was owned by a widow who did not want to move but had been told she could live on the property for two more years.

Next the three young detectives reached a retirement home for women. No vehicles were allowed beyond the fenced-in grounds, so Nancy parked outside.

The visitors gave their names to a gatekeeper and at his request Nancy stated her business. He made a brief telephone call, then waved them inside the grounds.

As the trio walked up a sweeping driveway, they came to a sweet-faced elderly woman seated under a tree. The girls smiled at her.

"I'm Mrs. Carten," she spoke up. "Have you come to visit someone at our lovely home?"

"Not exactly," Nancy replied. "We heard that this place is about to be sold. Where are you all to be moved?"

Tears trickled down the woman's cheeks. "It is worse than that. A man bought the mortgage from the bank and now he has foreclosed on the property. We will have to move at once. I don't know what will become of us."

The girls were dismayed to hear this. They

expressed their sympathy, then George asked, "Is the man's name Mr. Wright?"

"Yes, it is," Mrs. Carten answered.

Nancy suggested the girls talk to the owner, Mrs. Sutton. She found her seated at a desk in a large cheerful office. Mrs. Sutton confirmed the story.

"All of us who live here are heartbroken," she said.

"We're very sorry," Bess spoke up. "Has Mr. Wright actually foreclosed?"

"It can happen at any time," the woman replied.

The phone on her desk rang. Mrs. Sutton answered and in a moment drew in her breath. She put the phone down, then burst into tears.

"Forgive me, please," she said. "It has happened. Mr. Wright has given formal notice of a foreclosure."

"Perhaps I can help you," said Nancy. "May I make a call?" The woman nodded.

Nancy dialed her father's office. Quickly she told him where she was and what had happened. "Oh, Dad, please try to do something fast!"

CHAPTER XIX

Lost Loot

"I'LL see what I can do about the retirement home foreclosure at once!" Mr. Drew promised Nancy. "Suppose you go over to Thurstons and see how they're making out. I'll call you there."

Nancy turned to Mrs. Sutton and told her she hoped to have good news in a short time.

"Try not to worry," she begged her.

Nancy, Bess, and George said good-by and set off for the farm. Upon arriving they rang the front doorbell. Receiving no response, the three were worried that Mrs. Thurston might be alone and ill, so they walked in.

"Listen!" Bess said. "I hear Mrs. Thurston mumbling something."

Nancy called out hello but there was no answer. The girls walked into the living room. At one end sat Mrs. Thurston in her wheelchair.

She was alongside a table on which stood a cup

and saucer. The woman was gazing into it intently. Although the mumbling was louder and clearer now, the girls could not discern what she was saying.

"Tea leaves," Bess ventured.

Nancy had paused, uncertain what to do. She did not want to frighten Mrs. Thurston, who seemed to be in a trance. To her surprise the woman swung her wheelchair around and looked straight at the visitors.

"I knew you were coming," she said, smiling. "The tea leaves told me so."

George opened her mouth to make a retort, but was warned against speaking by a stern look from Nancy.

"Hello," the young detective said. "How are you feeling?"

Mrs. Thurston gave her usual answer, "Not very well." Then she added, "Your visit has been the first nice thing that has happened here today."

The girls said thank you and then waited for Mrs. Thurston to proceed.

"A little while ago Rausch was in here talking to me. Suddenly he looked out the open window over there and without saying a word stepped right through it. You know that brings bad luck. One should never step out of a window."

The remark struck Bess as funny. Giggling, she said, "Especially if it's a second-floor window."

Nancy and George laughed too, but Mrs.

Thurston saw nothing amusing about it. "The window Rausch left from has only a short drop. Oh, Oscar and I have had so many unfortunate things happen. Now I know there are going to be more!"

Nancy went to the woman's side and patted her shoulder. "Please try to think of pleasant things," the young detective said. "I'm sure that many of these premonitions of yours have never come true."

Mrs. Thurston had to admit this was correct but kept pointing out the recent bad luck they had had.

Nancy was curious to know why Rausch should have left the room so hurriedly and in such an eccentric way. She decided to find him. Nancy excused herself and hurried toward the cages at the rear of the house. Rausch was putting fresh water into a long trough for a flock of gaily colored parrots, white cockatoos, and green parakeets with dark-gray heads.

"Hi!" she called out. "Did something happen?"

The farmer's assistant looked up. "I'll say it did. I got here just in time to keep these birds from being poisoned."

"Poisoned!" Nancy exclaimed. "By whom?"

Rausch said he did not know but thought the culprit was probably Slick Fingers.

"While I was talking to Mrs. Thurston," he said, "I looked out the window. A man was sneaking along beside this cage. He had a watering can with a long spout and was pouring some dark-colored liquid into this trough."

Nancy was horrified. "How awful!" she cried out. "Are you sure you emptied out the poison before any of the birds took a drink?"

Rausch was positive because he had acted immediately. "I went in, grabbed up the trough, and ran outside with it," he explained. "I dumped the water far away. Then I took off after that fiend, but I didn't catch him. He disappeared toward the road."

Nancy remarked that Slick Fingers probably had a car parked there. "I'll look around," she said.

She took a magnifying glass from her skirt pocket and began to hunt for footprints or other clues to the intruder. In a few minutes she saw a white envelope lying partially under a bush. She picked it up and found that the envelope was sealed. There was no identifying mark of any kind on it.

"Considering how important every potential piece of evidence is in this case, I guess it would be all right for me to open it," the young detective rationalized.

Nancy slit open the envelope. Peering inside, she was amazed to see a large quantity of one hundred and five hundred dollar bills. There was also a smaller envelope. Nancy removed it.

"Oh!" she murmured.

On the front side was the now-familiar sign of the circle with the cross in the center!

Nancy wondered if Merv Marvel had had a hand in this. And was Slick Fingers working with him?

Nancy now opened the smaller envelope and stared unbelievingly. Inside lay several rings set with gorgeous gems.

"Stolen?" she wondered. "I must report my find to the police at once."

Nancy hurried back to the house. Rausch was not in sight so she could not tell him about the amazing discovery. She burst in upon Bess, George, and Mrs. Thurston and showed them what she had found. Next Nancy dashed to the telephone and called Chief Pepper.

The officer was thunderstruck by her report and started to praise the young detective. With a quick thank-you she went on, "Don't you think that the person who dropped the envelope will return to hunt for it?"

"No doubt about it. I'll send some men out there to capture him."

Chief Pepper requested Nancy to go at once to the spot where she had found the envelope and lay the large one, empty, back in place.

"Are you planning to stay at the farm?" he asked.

"At least until my father phones, but—" After

a pause she went on, "If it's all right, we'd like to see you catch Slick Fingers or anyone else who comes for the envelope."

"After you put it back, please stay in the house," the chief said firmly. "If anyone comes to call, keep him there. If we nab the suspect we'll blow a whistle, then you can come out."

Nancy ran to place the envelope near the bush, then dashed back to the house. When she relayed Chief Pepper's instructions to Bess, George, and Mrs. Thurston, she was surprised that the woman reacted so calmly to the tense situation.

Bess motioned for Nancy to come out to the kitchen. When the two girls reached it, she said excitedly, "I think George and I have talked Mrs. Thurston out of her superstitions and beliefs in omens and jinxes."

Nancy smiled. "If you've done that, you're both wonders. I guess our visits have had a good effect on her, after all."

She returned to the living room and the longer she talked with Mrs. Thurston, the more she became convinced that indeed Bess and George had accomplished a miracle. Mrs. Thurston joked and laughed and seemed genuinely excited over the thought of a thief being caught on their property, and she showed no anxiety about his presence.

A short while later Oscar returned from an

interview with Mr. Drew. He said Nancy's father had gathered important information from papers Mr. Thurston had forgotten about. They would greatly help his case against the High Rise company. When he finished telling the others, the bird owner suddenly turned to his wife.

She smiled at him and said, "Oscar, these girls have been a blessing in disguise to us. See how I've changed? I'm not worried any more!"

Oscar looked sober for a moment, then he beamed, crossed the room and kissed his wife fervently. "Thank goodness," he said.

The girls discreetly left the room and went to the kitchen to prepare some food. Later, while the group was eating, Mr. Drew called.

"Good news! I was able to get a postponement on that retirement home foreclosure."

"Great!" said Nancy. She now told him about the envelope she had found with the symbol on it and of Rausch's suspicion that Slick Fingers had tried to poison the parrots and other birds in the same cage.

"I certainly hope the thief returns and the police catch him," the lawyer said. "And now I have some interesting news for you, Nancy. Ned phoned me to say that he, Burt, and Dave had already uncovered several questionable practices that are being carried on by the High Rise Construction Company. They have been talking to employees. The boys are going to stay a while longer and see what else they can learn."

Before Nancy could comment, she heard a shrill police whistle. "Dad, I must go! Chief Pepper's men are here! They must have captured the thief!"

She hurriedly said good-by and rejoined Bess and George. The three girls, followed by Oscar, dashed off to the area where Nancy had found the telltale envelope.

When they reached it, the suspect was surrounded by four officers. He was indeed Slick Fingers, who was proclaiming loudly that he knew nothing about the envelope—that he was merely hiking through the woods.

When the girls ran up to him, Nancy pulled out the evidence which she had kept in a pocket. One of the officers identified the jewelry as a recent theft from a local store.

"I didn't steal it!" Slick Fingers shouted, but when he saw the money he became emotional and exclaimed, "That's mine! Give it back!"

The police stared at him. "I guess that's enough of a confession," one of them said. "Come along!"

The parolee did not move. Instead he looked directly at Nancy. Then, acting like a wild man, he screamed and yelled at her.

"You're responsible for all my bad luck. You ought to be locked up! You're nothing but a troublemaker! I hate you!"

An officer grabbed the man firmly by an arm. "That's all. Come with me."

"May I ask him a question?" Nancy requested the policeman.

"Go ahead. He's been advised of his constitutional rights."

"How did you know about the symbol of the circle with the cross in it?" she asked the prisoner. "And what's your connection with Merv Marvel?"

Slick Fingers showed agitation and looked at the ground, but he did not answer. Finally he was taken away by the officers.

It was dusk when Oscar and the girls returned to the house. Mrs. Thurston had lighted the lamps and was anxiously waiting for them. She was overjoyed to hear of the capture. Nancy went to the phone and called her father. He too expressed delight at the outcome.

Nancy said, "If we could only find Merv Marvel, we could probably close the case."

Her father agreed. Nancy said she had a hunch the dancer might pay a visit to the farm. "Mr. Wright may even send him here to carry on Slick Fingers' work."

After she had finished talking with her father, Nancy mentioned this to Oscar. He begged the girls to stay there in case Merv Marvel should show up. As they went outside with him to feed the birds, Kammy returned and was told of Slick Fingers' capture.

"I am glad," she said. "Did he confess to stealing the wryneck from the museum?" Nancy told her that the man had not.

After the chores were finished, they all went back into the house. Bess and George thought perhaps the girls should leave, but again Oscar prevailed upon them to stay longer. Marking time made Nancy fidgety. Finally to calm her nervousness, she went outside to walk around.

As she neared the bird enclosures, she saw a tall, slim man sneaking along close to the rear of one cage.

Impulsively she dashed after him. "What do you think you're doing?" she demanded.

He whirled, surprised.

"Who are you?" Nancy asked firmly.

He gave an odd smile. "My name is Merv Marvel," he said softly.

The next moment he swooped her up in his arms and held a hand over her mouth so she could not scream. Taking great leaps, he carried the helpless girl away from the Thurston farm!

CHAPTER XX

A Spook Unspooked

NANCY struggled with all the strength she could muster to free herself from Merv Marvel's arms. But the tall, handsome dancer had muscles as strong as steel and held her tightly. His long, powerful leaps and running steps soon carried the two of them far away from the Thurston farmhouse.

Finally he set Nancy down in a field, but maintained a viselike grip on one arm. "You little vixen!" he exclaimed. "You may as well stop fighting because you're not going to leave me. I'll teach you to be my dancing partner."

The strange remark frightened Nancy. She had hoped Merv Marvel would tire of the game he seemed to be playing and release her. Now she decided he was a bit unbalanced and could not be reasoned with.

Nancy stood still and murmured, "All right, I'll behave. Now let's go back."

"Oh no," Merv said. "We're going to dance."

An idea came to Nancy. Maybe he was staying with a group who used the circle-and-cross symbol, and she could go there with him and solve this mystery!

"Okay," she said. "It will be fun to dance. Will you take me to your headquarters?"

Merv Marvel stared at her. "What headquarters?"

With one foot Nancy sketched out a circle and put a full-sized cross in the middle of it.

Merv was startled. "You—you know about our headquarters?" He did not wait for a reply but said, "Yes, we will go there." He took her hand and together they began to waltz as he whistled softly.

"Now we'll leap!" he said.

Still holding her hand tightly, he waited for an upbeat in the tune, then the pair made a flying swing through the air.

"You're great!" Merv told her. "We'll ask the Grand Master to arrange a program for us."

Nancy's heart skipped a beat. Had she deliberately put herself into a situation from which it might be impossible to retreat? She quickly changed the subject.

"Do you play spook for the people at headquarters?" she asked.

"No, of course not," he replied. Then, as the full meaning of her question struck him, he asked,

"How did you know I sometimes play spook?"

Nancy described how he had frightened Mrs. Thurston and tried to frighten the Tabler grandchildren into believing a lot of foolish superstitions.

"You know too much," the dancer said.

"Who hired you to play spook?" Nancy prodded him.

Merv was not taken off guard. "You already know who it was and I'm not going to work for him any more. Mr. Wright isn't honest and he gets other people to do his dirty work for him."

Nancy was thrilled at the progress of her inquiries. "Yes, he hired both you and Slick Fingers."

Merv admitted this but denied having done anything except play spook. He accused Slick Fingers, however, of stealing a wryneck from the Harper University Museum and trying to scare Nancy with it.

"Later Slick took some valuable birds from there too. He also inoculated one of Mr. Thurston's birds with a virus and, of course, the others caught it," Merv said.

Nancy remarked, "And he used chloroform to knock out Mr. Thurston and Ned Nickerson."

Once again Merv said yes, but he denied any knowledge of the theft of the live wryneck Petra.

"I know something else, though," Merv said. "Mr. Wright asked Mr. Hinchcliff's son to annoy your friends if he had a chance, and he pushed a supermarket cart into you, but it was the boy's own idea to throw ink and glue at the other girls while they were at the newspaper office. Well, here we go. Leap!"

Nancy performed as requested. Now she could see dim lights in an old barn a short distance ahead. Merv took her directly there. Suddenly all the illumination went out and total silence followed.

Merv stopped moving but still held Nancy's hand tightly. A few moments later they heard weird music on high-pitched, plaintive mid-Eastern instruments. It was accompanied by chanting. The lights were switched on again.

Nancy and Merv looked inside the barn. The walls were decorated with Oriental and African masks. The circle-and-cross symbol had been painted everywhere. Strange-looking people were doing an exotic, slow dance with convulsive twists and snakelike turns.

"It's the devil dance!" Merv told Nancy. "We'll go in."

He shoved her toward a guard at the door. The man was tall, muscular-looking, and wore a European sixteenth-century suit of armor, but instead of a helmet, his head was covered with a turban from which protruded a long willowy gray feather.

He grabbed Nancy's wrist and hissed into her ear, "We're going to make a witch of you!"

The musicians stopped playing abruptly. Merv said to her, "The Grand Master is ready for new members!" He led Nancy forward.

Sometime after Nancy had been kidnapped, Ned, Burt, and Dave arrived at the Thurston farmhouse. The boys found everyone there frantic over Nancy's disappearance. A quick search of the grounds had been made, then the police had been called.

Chief Pepper came in a short while with three officers. By now it was dark. The police focused a powerful searchlight on an area where a man's foot had stomped down hard. The police found the matching print some distance away, then another.

Bess and George conferred. Had the leaping male ballet dancer been there?

On inspiration George hurried inside the house and telephoned the theater where the ballet performances were being held.

She asked, "Would it be possible for me to speak to Boris Borovsky?"

When he came to the phone, George explained what had occurred and the suspicion that Merv Marvel might have taken Nancy away.

"If so, can you give us any clue to where?"

Boris was able to offer one fact. Merv Marvel was very much interested in witchcraft.

"He might be a member of some demoniac

group. I wish I could be of more help, and I hope you find Nancy Drew. She's a wonderful girl and I wouldn't want anything to happen to her."

George thanked Boris for his suggestion and then returned to the others. She related what she had learned. The police did not know of any meeting place for a witchcraft group but would start a search.

All this while Ned had been conducting his own examination of the grounds. He pointed out that there were no tire tracks except those made by Oscar's station wagon.

"The kidnapper must have come and left on foot. Maybe if we look some more, we can find out which direction he took."

Again the officers played their searchlights over the area. Nancy's and Merv's footprints were picked up and led the searchers to the old barn. As they drew closer to it, all the lights went out.

The rescue party listened. Then from within came the hoot of an owl—the secret distress signal used by Nancy, Bess, and George!

"She's in there!" Bess cried out.

At once the police turned all their searchlights on the barn. People in weird costumes began scurrying from every exit.

"Nancy! Nancy!" Ned cried out, dashing toward the barn, with the others at his heels.

A moment later Nancy appeared. Seeing her friends, she ran toward them.

"You're safe!" Ned exclaimed as she fell into his outstretched arms.

Nancy looked for the police. Finding an officer, she said to him, "Come quick! You must arrest the Grand Master. He is a fake and cons money out of all these people. Merv Marvel is one of the victims. Besides, I think he needs psychiatric treatment. You'd better take him along."

She and her friends now left and the police took charge in the barn. Nancy and the others slowly walked back across the fields to the Thurston farmhouse. As they entered it, the phone was ringing.

Mr. Drew was calling Nancy to say that sufficient evidence had been collected against Ramsey Wright and the other executives in his company to bring about their arrest for fraud and coercing people into selling to him cheap the property they owned.

"Incidentally, he financed the witchcraft setup as a little private moneymaking project."

"This really is news!" said Nancy.

Oscar had come to say a word himself. "Mr. Drew, could you join us out here? I think the successful conclusion of this case calls for a celebration."

Mr. Drew agreed. While they were waiting for him, Mrs. Thurston, apparently fully recovered and gay and happy, helped Bess and George prepare a snack.

Nancy had gone off to wash her face and hands, comb her hair, and sit down to rest for a few minutes. The various angles of the mystery ran through her mind like a kaleidoscope.

Then suddenly she sat up straight, thinking, "The part involving Kammy hasn't been solved!"

She went at once to find the Eurasian girl. Kammy was in her room saying something softly to Petra in her native tongue.

"Kammy," said Nancy, "you once promised to tell me a story about yourself and your life. Could you do so now? It may explain some of the points in the mystery which haven't been cleared up."

Kammy smiled and the two girls sat down on the bed side by side.

"The wryneck in our country," Kammy began, "is almost a sacred bird. In ancient times it was used to try bewitching people who were interfering with royalty. My ancestors belonged to the royal family, and even though the country is no longer a kingdom, we descendants have always kept a wryneck with us."

The Eurasian girl said that after arriving at the university she had become acquainted with an American boy. "He turned out not to be a friend, and I was too embarrassed to talk about it. He liked to play jokes. After I told him I did not care to see him any longer, he began to annoy me in all sorts of ways.

"One time when we were studying together I had idly drawn the magical symbol of the circle with the wide cross inside it. He thought this was very funny and later whenever he saw a chance teased me about it."

Nancy asked, "Was he the one who put the jinx symbol inside Ned's car and in your theme papers?"

Kammy nodded. "And he is the one who stole Petra and also took my ring, which he taped underneath the bird's wing."

"Did you ever speak to him about it?"

"Indeed, yes," Kammy said, her dark eyes flashing. "His reply was that he was sure the bird would come back to me. He was only playing a joke."

"Kammy," said Nancy, giving her new friend a kiss, "please forgive us all for having been suspicious of you from time to time. I realize now why you felt you could not tell us your story."

The two girls stood up, smiled broadly at each other, then went downstairs. Mr. Drew had just arrived and the whole group sat around the living room enjoying the snack and swapping stories about the mystery. As often happened when Nancy finished work on a case, she began to wonder what the next one would be. It proved to be a highly exciting adventure, *Mystery of the Glowing Eye*.

She was brought back to the present as her father surprised everyone by an announcement. "Just before I left the house," he said, "I had a phone call from Chief Pepper. He told me that each of the five councilmen wanted Nancy Drew to know that they had voted to award the building contract to another company and to accept her plan for the complex of apartment houses.

"Oscar, you are to stay here. Your property will not be condemned and you will not have to sell."

A great shout of delight went up from the listeners and tears of joy filled the eyes of both Oscar and his wife Martha.

"You are such wonderful people," Oscar said. "I—we—"

He found it difficult to finish. Nancy relieved him of having to say anything more. Grinning, she declared:

"I forgot to tell you all that the Grand Master at that strange barn actually dubbed me a witch. Somebody had better unjinx me double-quick!"

Own the original 58 action-packed

HARDY BOYS MYSTERY STORIES®

In *hardcover* at your local bookseller OR
Call 1-800-788-6262, and start your collection today!

All books priced @ $5.99

1	The Tower Treasure	0-448-08901-7	32	The Crisscross Shadow	0-448-08932-7
2	The House on the Cliff	0-448-08902-5	33	The Yellow Feather Mystery	0-448-08933-5
3	The Secret of the Old Mill	0-448-08903-3	34	The Hooded Hawk Mystery	0-448-08934-3
4	The Missing Chums	0-448-08904-1	35	The Clue in the Embers	0-448-08935-1
5	Hunting for Hidden Gold	0-448-08905-X	36	The Secret of Pirates' Hill	0-448-08936-X
6	The Shore Road Mystery	0-448-08906-8	37	The Ghost at Skeleton Rock	0-448-08937-8
7	The Secret of the Caves	0-448-08907-6	38	Mystery at Devil's Paw	0-448-08938-6
8	The Mystery of Cabin Island	0-448-08908-4	39	The Mystery of the Chinese Junk	0-448-08939-4
9	The Great Airport Mystery	0-448-08909-2	40	Mystery of the Desert Giant	0-448-08940-8
10	What Happened at Midnight	0-448-08910-6	41	The Clue of the Screeching Owl	0-448-08941-6
11	While the Clock Ticked	0-448-08911-4	42	The Viking Symbol Mystery	0-448-08942-4
12	Footprints Under the Window	0-448-08912-2	43	The Mystery of the Aztec Warrior	0-448-08943-2
13	The Mark on the Door	0-448-08913-0	44	The Haunted Fort	0-448-08944-0
14	The Hidden Harbor Mystery	0-448-08914-9	45	The Mystery of the Spiral Bridge	0-448-08945-9
15	The Sinister Signpost	0-448-08915-7	46	The Secret Agent on Flight 101	0-448-08946-7
16	A Figure in Hiding	0-448-08916-5	47	Mystery of the Whale Tattoo	0-448-08947-5
17	The Secret Warning	0-448-08917-3	48	The Arctic Patrol Mystery	0-448-08948-3
18	The Twisted Claw	0-448-08918-1	49	The Bombay Boomerang	0-448-08949-1
19	The Disappearing Floor	0-448-08919-X	50	Danger on Vampire Trail	0-448-08950-5
20	Mystery of the Flying Express	0-448-08920-3	51	The Masked Monkey	0-448-08951-3
21	The Clue of the Broken Blade	0-448-08921-1	52	The Shattered Helmet	0-448-08952-1
22	The Flickering Torch Mystery	0-448-08922-X	53	The Clue of the Hissing Serpent	0-448-08953-X
23	The Melted Coins	0-448-08923-8	54	The Mysterious Caravan	0-448-08954-8
24	The Short-Wave Mystery	0-448-08924-6	55	The Witchmaster's Key	0-448-08955-6
25	The Secret Panel	0-448-08925-4	56	The Jungle Pyramid	0-448-08956-4
26	The Phantom Freighter	0-448-08926-2	57	The Firebird Rocket	0-448-08957-2
27	The Secret of Skull Mountain	0-448-08927-0	58	The Sting of the Scorpion	0-448-08958-0
28	The Sign of the Crooked Arrow	0-448-08928-9			
29	The Secret of the Lost Tunnel	0-448-08929-7		*Also available*	
30	The Wailing Siren Mystery	0-448-08930-0		The Hardy Boys Detective Handbook	0-448-01990-6
31	The Secret of Wildcat Swamp	0-448-08931-9		The Bobbsey Twins of Lakeport	0-448-09071-6

VISIT PENGUIN PUTNAM BOOKS FOR YOUNG READERS ONLINE:
http://www.penguinputnam.com

We accept Visa, Mastercard, and American Express.
Call 1-800-788-6262

Own the original 56 thrilling

NANCY DREW MYSTERY STORIES®

In *hardcover* at your local bookseller OR
Call 1-800-788-6262, and start your collection today!

All books priced @ $5.99

The Secret of the Old Clock	0-448-09501-7	
The Hidden Staircase	0-448-09502-5	
The Bungalow Mystery	0-448-09503-3	
The Mystery at Lilac Inn	0-448-09504-1	
The Secret of Shadow Ranch	0-448-09505-X	
The Secret of Red Gate Farm	0-448-09506-8	
The Clue in the Diary	0-448-09507-6	
Nancy's Mysterious Letter	0-448-09508-4	
The Sign of the Twisted Candles	0-448-09509-2	
Password to Larkspur Lane	0-448-09510-6	
The Clue of the Broken Locket	0-448-09511-4	
The Message in the Hollow Oak	0-448-09512-2	
The Mystery of the Ivory Charm	0-448-09513-0	
The Whispering Statue	0-448-09514-9	
The Haunted Bridge	0-448-09515-7	
Clue of the Tapping Heels	0-448-09516-5	
Mystery of the Brass-Bound Trunk	0-448-09517-3	
The Mystery of the Moss-Covered Mansion	0-448-09518-1	
The Quest of the Missing Map	0-448-09519-X	
The Clue in the Jewel Box	0-448-09520-3	
The Secret in the Old Attic	0-448-09521-1	
The Clue in the Crumbling Wall	0-448-09522-X	
Mystery of the Tolling Bell	0-448-09523-8	
The Clue in the Old Album	0-448-09524-6	
The Ghost of Blackwood Hall	0-448-09525-4	
The Clue of the Leaning Chimney	0-448-09526-2	
The Secret of the Wooden Lady	0-448-09527-0	
The Clue of the Black Keys	0-448-09528-9	
Mystery at the Ski Jump	0-448-09529-7	
The Clue of the Velvet Mask	0-448-09530-0	

31	The Ringmaster's Secret	0-448-09531-9
32	The Scarlet Slipper Mystery	0-448-09532-7
33	The Witch Tree Symbol	0-448-09533-5
34	The Hidden Window Mystery	0-448-09534-3
35	The Haunted Showboat	0-448-09535-1
36	The Secret of the Golden Pavilion	0-448-09536-X
37	The Clue in the Old Stagecoach	0-448-09537-8
38	The Mystery of the Fire Dragon	0-448-09538-6
39	The Clue of the Dancing Puppet	0-448-09539-4
40	The Moonstone Castle Mystery	0-448-09540-8
41	The Clue of the Whistling Bagpipes	0-448-09541-6
42	The Phantom of Pine Hill	0-448-09542-4
43	The Mystery of the 99 Steps	0-448-09543-2
44	The Clue in the Crossword Cipher	0-448-09544-0
45	The Spider Sapphire Mystery	0-448-09545-9
46	The Invisible Intruder	0-448-09546-7
47	The Mysterious Mannequin	0-448-09547-5
48	The Crooked Banister	0-448-09548-3
49	The Secret of Mirror Bay	0-448-09549-1
50	The Double Jinx Mystery	0-448-09550-5
51	Mystery of the Glowing Eye	0-448-09551-3
52	The Secret of the Forgotten City	0-448-09552-1
53	The Sky Phantom	0-448-09553-X
54	The Strange Message in the Parchment	0-448-09554-8
55	Mystery of Crocodile Island	0-448-09555-6
56	The Thirteenth Pearl	0-448-09556-4

Also available

The Bobbsey Twins of Lakeport	0-448-09071-6